It Happened One Winter

by
Christi Caldwell

Other Titles by Christi Caldwell

All the Duke's Sins
One for My Baron
It Had to Be the Duke
Along Came a Lady

Scandalous Affairs
A Groom of Her Own
Taming of the Beast
My Fair Marchioness
It Happened One Winter

Heart of a Duke
In Need of a Duke—Prequel Novella
For Love of the Duke
More than a Duke
The Love of a Rogue
Loved by a Duke
To Love a Lord
The Heart of a Scoundrel
To Wed His Christmas Lady
To Trust a Rogue
The Lure of a Rake
To Woo a Widow
To Redeem a Rake
One Winter with a Baron
To Enchant a Wicked Duke
Beguiled by a Baron
To Tempt a Scoundrel
To Hold a Lady's Secret
To Catch a Viscount

The Heart of a Scandal
In Need of a Knight—Prequel Novella
Schooling the Duke
A Lady's Guide to a Gentleman's Heart

A Matchmaker for a Marquess
His Duchess for a Day
Five Days with a Duke

Lords of Honor
Seduced by a Lady's Heart
Captivated by a Lady's Charm
Rescued by a Lady's Love
Tempted by a Lady's Smile
Courting Poppy Tidemore

Scandalous Seasons
Forever Betrothed, Never the Bride
Never Courted, Suddenly Wed
Always Proper, Suddenly Scandalous
Always a Rogue, Forever Her Love
A Marquess for Christmas
Once a Wallflower, at Last His Love

Sinful Brides
The Rogue's Wager
The Scoundrel's Honor
The Lady's Guard
The Heiress's Deception

The Wicked Wallflowers
The Hellion
The Vixen
The Governess
The Bluestocking
The Spitfire

The Theodosia Sword
Only For His Lady
Only For Her Honor
Only For Their Love

Danby
A Season of Hope
Winning a Lady's Heart

The Brethren
The Spy Who Seduced Her
The Lady Who Loved Him
The Rogue Who Rescued Her
The Minx Who Met Her Match
The Spinster Who Saved a Scoundrel

Lost Lords of London
In Bed with the Earl
In the Dark with the Duke
Undressed with the Marquess

Brethren of the Lords
My Lady of Deception
Her Duke of Secrets

The Read Family Saga
A Winter Wish

Regency Duets
Rogues Rush In: Tessa Dare and Christi Caldwell
Yuletide Wishes: Grace Burrowes and Christi Caldwell

Her Christmas Rogue

Standalone
Fighting for His Lady

Memoir: Non-Fiction
Uninterrupted Joy

It Happened One Winter
Copyright © 2021 by Christi Caldwell
Print Edition

All rights reserved. No part of this story may be reproduced in any form by any electronic or mechanical means—except in the case of brief quotations embodied in critical articles or reviews—without written permission.

The characters and events portrayed in this book are fictitious. Any similarity to real persons, living or dead, is purely coincidental and not intended by the author.

For more information about the author:
www.christicaldwellauthor.com
christicaldwellauthor@gmail.com
Twitter: @ChristiCaldwell
Or on Facebook at: Christi Caldwell Author

About the Book

Mr. Martin Phippen, a highly successful London builder, is forced by a business partner's foolish decision, to take on a project in the wretchedly scenic wilds of Yorkshire. Three little scamps have made his work site their private playground, and Martin is determined that their mischief be curtailed before somebody gets badly hurt. Widowhood means Mrs. Christina Thacker has her hands full with her children, while her exchequer is distressingly empty. To remedy her lack of funds, she focuses on making a match at her sister's upcoming house party. When Christina's energies should be fixed on finding security for her family, she is instead powerfully drawn to the blunt, irascible Londoner with callused hands, sharp wit… and also, an intrinsic honor. As passions flare between Christina and Martin, she must choose between a future defined by predictable security, or one built—with Martin—on a foundation of love.

Chapter 1

North Yorkshire, England
Winter 1829

Martin Phippen was under attack.

And as one of London's premier builders, it certainly wasn't the first time he'd contended with outside threats to either his investments or projects.

But these foes were decidedly the most resolute... and ruthless.

Another rock burst through the window, exploding one of the few remaining uncracked panes in this new property he'd purchased. Cursing, Martin lunged for the narrow spot of plaster between the windows. Still, glass sprayed him and around the room, raining down like the crystal snowflakes that hadn't quit since he'd gotten to Yorkshire.

Broken glass tinkled noisily upon the wood floors in desperate need of a varnish, or replacement, with an uneven, but steady *ping, ping, ping*.

And then... silence.

He stood there, his back pressed to the wall.

Plink.
Plink.
Plink.

Glaring, Martin took in the massacre made of glass by the mercenary lot outside. This had been the last room with fully intact windowpanes in the *great brick manor house*, as his brother had referred to it.

No more.

Someone outside had chosen to make target practice out of the remaining leaded glass in the house.

Though, in fairness, *great manor house*—or even for that matter, simply *house*—was a ludicrous descriptor for this *new property*. Both had been used interchangeably by his naïve partner, also his younger brother, a military man turned builder.

"New property," Martin muttered under his breath.

Seven years younger than Martin's thirty-five years, Thaddeus had joined Martin in his craft with the same zeal he'd used with the toy soldiers he'd battered against one another in the imagined play battles he'd orchestrated upon the uneven plank flooring of their family's house in the Rookeries.

Where Martin approached each project with cool-headed logic and an emotional detachment, Thaddeus always threw himself feet-first into any and every aspect of life. That had been the case when he'd signed up to serve in the king's army, and that had remained the case when he'd returned home, in search of work—work that Martin had, without hesitation, provided him with.

In terms of construction and renovation projects, there was no project too big or small.

And no property unsalvageable.

That was what Martin had always believed, too.

That was, in fact, the lesson he'd given his naïve and trusting brother. That had also apparently proved to be a lesson the younger man had taken to heart.

In so doing, Thaddeus had made a liar out of Martin in the advice he'd given about expecting something from nothing where any and all properties were concerned.

Silently cursing, Martin moved his gaze slowly around the empty parlor, taking in everything from the glass littering the warped and faded oak flooring to the cracked plaster.

The floor-to-ceiling windows, with every other one previously cracked and missing panes, had been thoroughly divested of the last intact panels.

Errant snowflakes carried into the room, gusted in by the winter wind. The flakes floated down to join the glass littering the floor, melting almost on impact so that the remnants of the melted flakes glistened upon those lead remains.

Plink.

As that last, solitary little cling of glass fell forlornly, joining the other shards throughout the room, Martin remained at the narrow place between the windows, waiting for another assault on his new properties... that did not come.

Since he'd arrived only last night, his journey from London slowed by a winter storm, he'd been largely unable to evaluate the state of his latest investment. As he'd been doused in darkness, freezing from the absence of a single fire, and completely abandoned, the main goal of last evening had been to not freeze to death.

There'd been no servants. Not a single one. A detail—an

important detail—his brother had failed to mention.

Family and business made dangerous bed partners. That's what he'd always heard. Familial loyalty, however, mattered more, and with his brother struggling financially to find his way since he'd returned from his time serving king and country abroad, there'd been no way Martin wouldn't hire the younger man.

Not for the first time since his arrival, however, he began to have his doubts about his brother's judgment on this particular *investment*.

A lone wind howled across the countryside. Spilling through the windows now devoid of glass panels, it whistled, a forlorn and haunting wail of nature protesting the unforgiveable harshness of an unexpectedly cold English winter.

Gritting his teeth to keep them from chattering, Martin finally relinquished his hiding place, stepped out into the room, and edged over to the nearest window. He surveyed the grounds, in search of the man responsible for—

A figure darted out from behind the towering trunk of an oak tree.

Martin opened his mouth to let fly another curse, trying to shift back from the window—too late.

A violent war whoop went up, echoing around a countryside made all the quieter by the early-morn hours and the latest blanket of snow that covered the earth, and that darting figure launched something with blindingly quick speed.

An ice-packed snowball exploded in a shimmery display, leaving crystalline remnants upon Martin's black wool jacket, a jacket he'd been forced to sleep in due to the cold of a crumbling estate in desperate need of repairs.

"Bloody hell," he snapped into the quiet.

That was really enough.

Stalking over to one of the paneless windows, Martin caught the sill and leaned out.

He immediately found the perpetrator behind the assault on his property.

Nay, not one.

Nor, for that matter, a man.

Rather, three small figures of varying ages.

Martin shifted his gaze over the three responsible for his rude morning wakeup and the attack. They were all dressed in coarse wool that, even with the ten paces between Martin and the trio, revealed age and wear. He moved his gaze past the boy tucked in the middle before swiftly jerking his stare over once more.

They were not all boys.

Granted, the smallest of the bunch wore boy's garments and could easily pass for one. Her dark hair, however, was a messy tangle down her back.

So *this* was who was responsible.

Children at play.

Some of the tension went out of his frame.

The local village children had likely assumed the properties remained uninhabited and had made it a source of target practice.

Just then, the little girl shot an arm up and waved excitedly.

One of the boys, with like coloring and similar features—likely a brother—shot an elbow into her side and said something.

Instantly contrite, the girl let her arm fall, folding her little limbs across her middle, and stared back at Martin with an impressive modicum of mutiny from one so young.

Martin leaned out another fraction, the sough of his breath leaving a cloud of white in the morning air. "No need to worry," he called down. "I trust you didn't expect anyone was living—"

The words died in the frigid air as the tallest of the boys drew his arm swiftly back and launched another snowball.

Cursing, Martin edged back.

But the boy proved too quick, or Martin proved too slow.

Oomph.

A perfectly packed and extremely hard snowball hit him in the nose, which proceeded to spurt blood.

Martin caught the wounded appendage and glared around his hand at the sniggering boys and the round-eyed girl, who at last managed to show the proper amount of fear.

Each boy took the pant-wearing little girl by a hand, and the children raced off together, their pace uneven as their small legs made the trudge through the deep-for-them snow.

Martin glared at their retreating forms.

The bloody savages.

One of the little boys glanced back and made a crude gesture.

Martin narrowed his eyes.

They were children.

They were just children.

He reminded himself of that detail to ease the simmering fury inside. Naughty, mischievous, troublemaking children. With his elder brother having two imps of his own, Martin knew something about the sort.

Granted, this lot of troublemakers had launched a full-scale attack upon his brother's latest investment, which, with its already-precarious state, was guaranteed to see Martin in the damned hole for the project.

Martin pinched his still-bleeding nose harder.

But still, children.

Martin briefly closed his eyes, reminding himself of that important reminder—they were just children. They—

Another snowball hit him.

They had returned.

He dove out of the way as they launched a second attack upon him.

Nay, these were not *children*. They were damned monsters.

A man had to draw the proverbial line somewhere.

Releasing a bellow, which was met by a flurry of gasps, he took off running down the uneven stairs that had been stripped bare of carpet at some point, its marks still left upon the wood.

The house was doused in darkness still, due to the lack of candles and the need to conserve fuel, as he headed toward the back of the manor house.

Scattered along the floor were details he'd failed to notice upon last evening's late arrival. Rocks—small ones, uneven ones, larger ones—littered the ground, the glass upon the floor indicating that his new investment had been used for target practice far longer than just the morning snowball assault.

Another wave of fury whipped through him.

Shoving the double doors of the terrace open, he stalked outside and down the snow-packed terrace.

Not that they would be here still.

Even with the distance between him and that trio, he'd caught the spark of fear before they'd darted to the copse.

Martin reached the crumbling banister that overlooked the back of his new properties. Gripping the ledge, he glared out.

In fairness, by the information his brother had obtained from their seller and the state of the manor itself, the crew of mischief makers had undoubtedly assumed the properties had been abandoned. Making his presence known beyond the murky shadow in the windows he'd been to the children that morning would prove the wisest way to establish the fact of ownership. Once they saw a person lived here, they'd likely find their trouble someplace else.

They—

His gaze snagged on the three children. Emerging from the copse with more of their war whoops, they burst forward through the snow.

Martin stilled. "You have got to be kidding me," he whispered into the morning still effectively broken by the antics of children who were either fearless or missing brains in their heads.

The tallest of the boys—the one with the impressive arm—wound his arm several times, as if he were in the middle of a competitive cricket match, and launched another snowball.

This time, Martin dodged the missile, and it sailed past, the slight crunch of snow and ice as it exploded upon the ground filtering through the air.

Collective groans went up among them, but the little girl bent, scooped herself up a small snowball, and hurled it, though ineffectually.

It appeared Martin had found himself three interlopers who'd no intention of quitting.

Turning on his heel, Martin strode the remainder of the terrace and, holding the railing, took the stairs quickly, the snow mounds upon the stone steps making his place slow and his gait awkward.

"You three," he bellowed, and either his nearness or the sound of his shout caused the trio to freeze. Using that shock to his advantage, he trudged on ahead. As he reached them, they appeared to find themselves—too late. With the girl and the smaller boy darting in opposite directions, Martin caught the tallest boy, the greatest offender, by the back of his jacket.

"Freeze," he said, releasing the child, even though he expected him to take flight.

Instead, the boy remained there, arms folded mutinously at his chest. From the corner of his eye, Martin spied the two other children reluctantly returning and taking up places on the other side of him.

By their similar coloring and freckled features, they were siblings.

"Well?" the tallest boy demanded. "What do you want?" He spoke in the crisp, condescending, cultured tones of quality and elevated birthright, the kind of tones Martin had grown accustomed to having turned his way by people who deemed themselves his betters.

He opened his mouth to tell the fancy-born child precisely what he thought of him and his uncouth manners, but then stopped, again noting the sorry state of the child's garments.

Martin moved his gaze down the line.

All three of them.

A little tug on Martin's sleeve brought his gaze down to the tiny girl. "Are you going to put him in the ribbet, sir?" she whispered, staring up at him with tears and fear brimming in her eyes, and damned if he didn't feel a chink in the fury that had sent him after them.

He shook his head confusedly. "The ribbet?"

"The gibbet," the smaller boy clarified, exasperation rich in his equally crisp King's English. "Luna means the gibbet."

All sadness and fear instantly receded from the girl. She glared at the one who'd explained for her. "I said gibbet, Logan. He heard me wrong."

"Did me and Lachlan hear you wrong, too?" Logan snapped back.

Just like that, the trio who'd had their sights set that morn on Martin and his properties turned on one another.

A melee spiraled quickly, with each child's words rolling over the others', their voices rising. Martin's temples started to throb from the quarreling that moved from them casting aspersions on one another's hearing and speech to the decision that saw them facing the "ribbet" and circled back to the original misspoken word that had landed them in the heart of their argument.

Their shouts escalated, and then Lachlan charged at his brother.

Oh, bloody hell.

"Enough," Martin bellowed, stepping between the combative boys. He stretched his arms wide to keep them from attacking each other, but the eldest went hurtling around Martin, evading his reach, and launched himself at his brother.

The smaller boy went flying into the snow.

Tamping down a groan, Martin immediately plucked the bigger child off his brother, and holding him gently but firmly at the nape of his garment, he prevented him from continuing the attack.

"You're bleeeeeeding," Luna cried and then promptly burst into tears.

Another cry went up, this time from across the lawns. "You monster!"

Yes, yes, they were.

Martin, along with the three children, turned his head in time to see the whirling bundle of fury barreling down on them. Clutching at her skirts as she trudged through the snow, the woman heading toward them took giant, awkward steps. All the while, her muffled, distant mutterings reached Martin.

"Mama does not walk well in the snow," Luna explained, just as the woman went pitching forward.

Squawking like a bird, Mama flapped her arms and somehow managed to keep her balance.

"I… see that," he said from the corner of his mouth.

Thank God. The mother. He followed her approach, never more grateful to see another person in his life.

"It's because she has big skirts on," Logan defended.

"And because she's angry," Lachlan added.

As she should be. If ever a group of children had deserved a maternal lecture, this trio was it.

At last, huffing and out of breath, the lady reached them.

She shoved back her deep black wool hood, revealing dark curls and a pair of blue eyes even wider than the daughter's. They were the captivating kind, when Martin wasn't one to be captivated by... anything. That was, anything beyond his own work. They were made even more enormous by the pale hue of her cheeks, splotched with circles of red from the cold. A fire glimmered in those aquamarine pools.

"You monster," she snapped for a second time. "Are you all right?" She directed that question at Lachlan, who in the melee with his brother had secured himself a bloody nose. The lady pressed her sleeve against the dripping appendage.

Martin frowned. Their family affairs weren't his business, and yet, it still bore pointing out. "They're both monsters." A slight tug at his sleeve brought his gaze down to Luna.

"Ahem." The little girl cleared her throat.

"They're *all* monsters," he corrected, and she smiled and nodded her approval at being included—as she'd deserved—in his count.

The young woman gasped. "How dare you?"

He furrowed his brow. Wait a moment.

How dare *he*?

And then it hit Martin as hard as the ice-packed snowballs her heathens of offspring had struck him with that morning. He reeled. "You're calling *me* a monster?" he demanded, because it really bore repeating.

"Well, how should I refer to a man who goes about attacking and scaring children?"

Attacking and scaring children?

All three children shared a smirk.

Nay, it was official—the woman was as mad as her misbehaving brood.

Chapter 2

Any man—nay, every man and certainly every woman would have felt a healthy modicum of fear and unease at the sparkling rage that glinted from the tall, dark, imposing stranger's brown eyes. He was several inches past six feet and broader than many of the trees she'd passed on her way to get to her children.

But Christina wasn't most women.

She was a mother.

A widow.

A mother with three children. And she'd be damned if she'd cower before or back down from any man, even one as broad and beefy as the one before her.

"Did you hear me?" she demanded when he did nothing more than stare at her like she'd sprouted a second head.

"Are you mad?" he snapped.

Lachlan, Logan, and Luna all exchanged uneasy glances.

In fairness, there'd been any number of times since her husband had first fallen ill, and then died, when she had felt like she'd descended into that state. Times when she'd found herself locked in her chambers with her head buried in a pillow as she'd screamed silently into the feather-stuffed article, over and over and over.

This time, however, was decidedly not one of them.

"I. Beg. Your. Pardon?" Christina asked, enunciating every single syllable.

"As you should." The stranger jerked his chin toward Lachlan, Logan, and Luna. "Along with your troublesome brood."

She sputtered. "My brood?"

"Your *troublesome* brood," he reiterated.

Christina rocked back. "Well, I never."

"Never taught them manners? Yes, I would say that."

And suddenly, all the frustration, all the annoyance with her circumstances, and all her patience—at having to be the perfect mother and having to constantly make excuses for her children to her own mother and everyone—snapped. Grabbing her hems and holding them aloft, Christina stalked forward and stopped when their boots touched. She immediately regretted that decision for the disadvantage it gave her. Craning her head back, she glared at the gentleman. "It is funny you should mention a lack of manners, because you, sir, are absent of them yourself and in desperate need of a lecture."

He narrowed his eyes. His thick, dark lashes swept down, giving him a menacing look. "Am I?"

Christina should have retreated at the cross between a silken purr and a growl—and undoubtedly would have at any other time.

Instead, she angled her head back farther and dropped her hands upon her hips. "Indeed, sir," she said. "Yelling loud enough to be heard through all of Yorkshire. Grabbing my children. Calling them monsters."

"Because they are."

It would have been less insulting had he snarled or hurled those words, rather than uttering them in the matter-of-fact way he had.

Christina glanced over at the three of her children who were present.

At the stranger's words, they hung their heads in a display of wounded affront so over the top that she as their mother was hard-pressed to believe it. She gritted her teeth hard enough that they clacked together. She knew precisely what her children were. It was, however, an entirely different thing hearing someone else speak so of them.

"Now, lady—"

"Mama isn't a lady," Luna piped in.

"Luna," she said warningly.

To no avail.

"Isn't she?" The stranger directed his interest and attention Luna's way.

"No. Mama is Mrs. Thacker. She married poor," her daughter went on with a rote rendition of one who'd heard those words spoken over and over. And she had. By Christina's mother. "And to a man without a title or anything of value to pass on to his—"

"That is enough, Luna," Christina said brusquely, and her daughter instantly fell silent.

Christina's mother still insisted that Christina's marrying outside the peerage and losing the title of *lady* had been the greatest tragedy. Which was saying much, given that Christina's father had coordinated the kidnapping of a young earl whose family had been struck down by fever so that he might assume the title of earl. The crime had gone unknown until just recently, when the world had discovered his involvement in it.

Lachlan cleared his throat. "Perhaps you should return to lecturing him, Mama?" Her eldest son's lower lip quivered. "He did scare us mightily."

With that, Christina whipped her furious gaze back over to the nasty brute. "Scaring children," she snapped, welcoming the sting of fury and upset on her children's behalf. "Yes, as I see it, there is only one monster present, sir."

Instead of releasing a bellicose shout, several of which he'd already produced that had shaken the countryside, he… chuckled.

It started as a low and deep rumble that faintly rocked his broad, powerful shoulders.

She thinned her eyes into slits. "Are you… laughing at me?"

At her side, she caught the uneasy looks her children exchanged.

"Uh-oh," Luna whispered. "Mr. Sir, you should be careful." The girl took pains to warn the imposing stranger. "Mama does not like it when we laugh when she's angry."

The finely attired gentleman looked to Luna. "Thanks for the information," he said on a less-than-discreet whisper, which he followed up with a little wink.

Christina faltered momentarily, knocked off-balance by the almost playful nature of the brute's exchange with her daughter.

Except, brutes didn't engage with little girls.

"Mama," Logan whispered, loud enough to recall the

stranger's attention. Her youngest son threw an elbow into Christina's side, pulling a grunt from her. "Aren't you going to yell at him?"

Yell at him?

She furrowed her brow.

Yes!

Of course.

"Yell at me, should she?" Gone was the gentle warmth the man had displayed for Luna. The hard gaze he trained on Logan sent Christina's son darting behind her.

Christina trembled briefly under that glint, which was frostier than the unforgivingly cold English morn. The gentleman honed his eyes on Christina, and refusing to cower, she steadied herself and lifted her chin another fraction.

"First," he began. "I'm no sir. I'm a mere mister. Mr. Martin Phippen, the property owner of this fine estate."

Cowardice drew her stare away from his, and she welcomed the reprieve to further steady herself, looking past him to the crumbling manor made of faded red brick that sun and time had since turned a faded shade of pink. Everything from the roof to the crumbling banisters and rails revealed age and disrepair. It would require time, funds, and a skilled builder to resurrect.

"Fine estate?" she murmured. And oddly, it was fine for the blank canvas it represented.

"Yes," he snapped. "Do you have a problem with that?"

Did she…?

Christina blinked several times. He'd taken her words as disparaging ones. "The only problem I have is with you coming after my children, Mr. Phippen. Instead of bothering with them, I'd suggest you spend time seeing to your windows." Turning a shoulder dismissively, she motioned for her children, who hastened onward with an alacrity she'd never seen from the trio, which was saying a good deal. She followed them.

"Do you mean the windows your angels shattered?" Mr. Phippen called after them, bringing Christina to a jarring halt.

Her children continued on without breaking stride. She stared at their rapidly retreating figures, and a pit born of horror formed in her belly.

For the first time since she'd come upon the dark, menacing figure with a hand on Lachlan's jacket, she faltered.

Luna sent a worried glance back over her shoulder at Christina. Nay, she wasn't worried, and that was when Christina knew.

Guilt.

Where Lachlan and Logan had become fairly adept at masking any and all guilt, a sentiment she didn't even know if they were capable of any longer, Luna remained an open book.

Christina briefly closed her eyes.

They'd done it.

They were responsible for the mess of his windows. Just as they'd been responsible for any series of messes and mischief at Claire and Caleb's properties. Yet again, Christina's only mildly mischievous children had become...

This was destructive, and rude, and dangerous—

Tears blurred her eyes, and battling an overwhelming

urge to both cry and scream, she quickened her steps, feeling the stranger—Mr. Phippen—staring after her.

God, what a blasted fool he must take her for.

Worse, she was a terrible mother who'd absolutely no idea the extent of the trouble her children had been up to.

What was even worse, a proper, respectable lady would have had the funds to compensate the man for the damage done to his property. But, God help her, Christina didn't have a pence to spare for proper garments, let alone some stranger's broken windows. Nay, she was the poor relation, a younger woman who relied upon the generosity of her younger sisters and eldest brother—

"Mama," Luna whispered as Christina, with the fast pace she'd set, hastened past her children.

Christina didn't even look back. "Not now," she said tightly, and her daughter went immediately silent.

Everything was falling apart.

Nay, everything had.

She could acknowledge that now.

Her breath came in noisy little spurts, uneven from the cold and the whir of panicky desperation and the pace she set.

It had all begun to unravel when her husband had fallen ill, and the time and limited monies Christina had had to spend upon her children had all instead gone to the care of Patrick.

But this? Christina gathered her increasingly heavy hem, sodden from the snow, higher and trudged ahead. This was worse.

"Is Mama all right?" Luna whispered.

"I… thinks so?" Lachlan returned his response in the form of a question and in the equally nervous tones evidenced in Luna's voice. At any other time, Christina would have immediately sought to put her children at ease and alleviate their fears.

But this time she couldn't.

Because she could not make it right, in any way.

A tear slipped down her cheek, the moisture warm upon her chilled skin, and she furiously brushed it back.

Nay, the only way to make this right was to marry again. Not for love, which she'd had before, but for wealth and security and stability for her and her children. That really had been the purpose of attending Claire and Caleb's current house party anyway—so that Christina could find a wealthy husband, one who wouldn't mind marrying a poor widow with not one, not two, not three, but four children, and who also came from a family with a scandalous history.

How difficult a feat could that be?

A panicky giggle gurgled in her throat as she picked up her pace, walking faster. And faster. Her skirts grew heavier from the snow soaking her hem line, and she wrested them higher and hurried onward.

Except her uneven motions tugged her back, and she overcompensated by propelling herself ahead.

Gasping, Christina lost her hold on her cloak and dress and went pitching forward. She shot her arms out to steady herself, but her efforts proved in vain.

She went flying, landing facedown in the snow.

With moisture seeping into her garments, chilling her from the inside out, and her face burning with pinpricks from the frigid snow, she found herself unable to get herself up. And she preferred the rest that came from lying down, blind to the whole world around her.

Chapter 3

Couldn't the young woman, with her tart mouth and misplaced fury, have just gone ahead and made her fiery march away *without* incident?

Couldn't the last exchange between them have died with her blind, delusional defense of her children?

Because there was something vastly different about seeing a shrew who'd defended her troublesome brood facedown in the snow, with those same, once-nasty buggers reduced to panic and worry all around her.

Cursing under his breath, Martin raced toward the lady, grinding up snow as he went, wetness seeping into his boots and infiltrating the heavy leather articles.

As one, the children looked up.

Gone from all their blue eyes was the devilish glimmer. In its place was fear. And worse, from the little girl, tears.

"She's d-dead," the girl—Luna, her mother had called her—whispered, her voice tremulous. A big, fat, lone teardrop ran down her cheek, and Martin's heart rent in two. "Just like Papa." At the exact moment those three words were uttered, a wind gusted, almost drowning out the forlorn pronouncement from the small child, but Martin had heard the words anyway.

Just like Papa.

That organ in his chest froze as the implications of that statement slammed into him.

His gaze went flying to the young woman, whom, with the Mrs. before her name, he'd taken for wed. Which she had been. She was too young to be a widow, certainly one with three young children.

But then, his sister's death all those years ago should have taught him that death made no exceptions when it came to snuffing out a life. Young or old, wealthy lords or impoverished street urchins, all were susceptible to its hand.

Martin bent a knee and reached to turn the young mother over just as her eldest son stretched a long branch out.

The boy poked the lady in her lower back.

"You're going to hurt her," Logan snapped.

"No, I'm not. She's dead. See?" Lachlan said, giving her another shove with that stick. "Told you both. Everyone dies."

With that, Luna burst into tears.

"I'm decidedly not dead." That muttered pronouncement emerged muffled, with the lady's face buried in the snow as it was. Still, however, she made no attempt to rise.

Instead, she seemed content to lie there.

As her children launched into triumphant war whoops that matched their cries when they'd attacked his new property, dancing a jig around their still-prone mother, he rather suspected why she lay the way she did.

These hellions were exhausting, and he'd known them for only a handful of minutes.

And they were apparently too young to be properly concerned about the fact that their mother made no attempt to rise.

Nay, instead, the youngest, Luna, began to sing a noisy song in time and in tune to "London Bridge Is Falling Down."

"Mama, Mama is aliiiiiiive. Is alive. Is aliiive. Mamaaa, Mama is alive, my fair Mamaaaa."

All the while, the boys proceeded to engage in a pretend battle, exchanging imagined blows with swords, using their motionless mother as the pretend victim of their savagery.

Was it a wonder the lady didn't want to get herself up to face this mayhem?

Muttering to himself, Martin reached past the sparring boys and skipping girl and plucked the lady from the ground.

Her face was a crisp, apple red from the cold, moisture clinging to her dark lashes, those enormous eyes made all the wider by the effects of the snow.

Her mouth parted a fraction, her generous lips forming a perfect moue, that lush flesh temptation itself. The kind that made a man forget himself.

Around them, the lady's children continued circling.

"Mamma, Mammma is standing up… standing up… standing up. Mamma… Mamma…"

The trio moved around him and the young woman like sharks rotating around prey, and the melee they made should have been distraction enough to break this powerful pull she had over him in this instant.

The young woman darted the tip of her tongue out and traced it along the wide seam of her lips, and he ripped his gaze away from the sight, the manner of which had led Adam to sin, and sin happily.

Except, his eyes collided with hers, and those irises proved as captivating.

When she'd first charged upon him, they'd been snapping with fury.

Which was why he was unnerved. Which was why he noticed.

That was the only reason, at all.

But so many shades of blue and tints of green and flecks of gold melded in them—

"Why are you looking at my mother like that?" Logan snapped, breaking the spell, and Martin wrenched his stare away from the young woman.

At some point, the trio had stopped their circling and lined up in a single, menacing line. The children looked upon Martin with suitable suspicion. That was, all of them but for the young sprite, who remained engrossed in a loose thread on the fingertip of her fraying gloves.

Lachlan shot a foot out, catching the little girl on her ankle.

"Ouch," Luna cried.

"Pay attention."

"I was, but I was tired of them staring at one another. That was no fun, and then I noticed my glove has a string, and I pulled it." Luna paused only long enough to stuff the article in question under her brother's nose and gather breath to continue speaking. "Why would I care that Mama is looking at him? That isn't fun."

An odd little strangled noise escaped said mother.

"And I don't care if he stares at Mama either." With a little shrug, the girl returned her scrutiny to her ancient leather gloves.

Martin gave thanks for the frigid cold of the winterscape that had already left his cheeks red and hopefully concealed his blush.

This was certainly a first.

He forced his gaze on the lady's sons and daughter, looking at anyone and anything except her.

Only, his focus snagged upon Luna's complete absorption in her gloves, the kidskin so tight upon those tiny digits that it made even small fingers appear large.

And he froze, this time for altogether different reasons.

At Luna's side, Lachlan nudged his chin up, angrily and mutinously. "You've got a problem with Luna's gloves?"

He shook his head in an automatic response. "I don't."

"Because they're old?" the other boy persisted, continuing over Martin's assurances.

"Lachlan," the boy's mother said tightly. A maternal warning as old as time, a tone he'd wager was inherent to all mothers everywhere, underscored the child's name.

"Or because they're falling apart?" Lachlan demanded.

"They aren't falling apart," Luna cried, and sticking her arm out, she gave it a shake, only highlighting the dangling strings and the little index finger poking through the small hole. "See?"

"What do you call that?" Lachlan shot back, jabbing angrily at the opening in the material.

"That is enough," Mrs. Thacker said.

The quarrel, however, continued, with the children raising their voices over one another.

Sticking his two middle fingers in his mouth, Martin let loose a piercing whistle that immediately cut across the cacophony.

The trio went silent.

"Your mother said enough," Martin said in quiet but stern tones that brought all three children's gazes falling to the snow. "Now, run along and pick up all the articles you dropped." They followed his gesture to the faded scarves and hats that littered the ground around them.

Logan pursed his mouth. "Who are you to order us about?" he asked, folding scrawny arms across an even more scrawny chest.

Martin leaned down the two feet separating them in height and put his nose against the boy's. "I'm the man whose household windows were shattered by you three."

Luna shot a hand up toward the sky and waggled it like a student eager to have her voice heard first.

He nudged his chin.

"I didn't break the windows, because I can't throw that far." The endearing little girl, with cherubic cheeks and dark brown curls like her mother, smiled a wide, dimpled grin, looking as pleased with herself as the cat who'd swallowed the canary.

Lachlan leaned around Martin. "But you *triiiied*." The boy squeezed several extra syllables into that overemphasized word.

Luna peeked around his other side and stuck her tongue out.

Her brother followed suit.

"Will you three just see to your things?" their mother entreated.

"What is he going to do if we don't?" the eldest boy taunted. "Make us pay? We don't have any money."

"Lachlan!" The young woman gasped out the child's name.

∽

Oh, God.

Would that the earth under her were, in fact, ice, and it could crack and swallow her whole.

This was awful. Agonizing and miserable.

Anything would be preferable to this.

She was unable to get a single word through the lump of humiliation that made it impossible to swallow or speak, but the tall, broad stranger at her side found his voice.

"Get going as your mother said," he said quietly, with more patience than her children deserved.

Her properly chastised children rushed off, leaving Christina and Martin alone.

And something in that grated.

They listened to him and not to her. As they'd ceased to listen to their father when he'd been too weak and sick to properly corral them. And this man would dare order her about.

They turned toward each other at the same time.

"I didn't need you to intervene."

He stared perplexedly at her, and she rushed to clarify.

"How dare you?" she exclaimed, cutting across whatever

reassuring words he'd been about to speak, leaving him with his broad jaw slack.

He quickly found his footing. His dark brows dipped in a way that would have menaced likely anyone else. "How dare I?"

Christina stood stiffly beside the bear of a man, rubbing her palms together to bring warmth to the cold digits. At her side, he was a tall fortress of a presence.

His features were slightly too heavy to ever be considered classically handsome. His jaw, square but wider than most, clefted slightly at the center. His nose was chiseled but bent, hinting at a break he'd suffered at some point. There was a rugged realness to him and his frame, and she... noticed him. It was the first time since her husband's passing that she'd noticed any man. In fact, it was the first time since she'd *met* her husband that she'd noticed anyone.

And she hated that it should be this one.

This man, who had seen exactly what her children were and called her out.

"You don't have to worry, Sunshine," he said in quiet tones for her alone. "I don't intend for them or you to pay."

She should be grateful, and yet, she could not be. Not when she was an object of pity among all—society, her family, and, worse, even this man, a stranger. And even as she knew it was wrong to take those frustrations out on this man, she could not stop the explosion. "I don't need your pity!" she said, her voice sharp.

He narrowed his eyes, and she paused, allowing a break for him to deny it, a denial that proved unforthcoming.

Despite the winter chill, her body burned with a blush.

The evidence of his restraint, coupled with the tenuous thread she had on her emotions, managed to calm her some.

"Furthermore," she said in a more even way, "although I appreciate your generosity in being willing to overlook the damage my children have done to your property, it is unnecessary." She brought her shoulders back and spoke in as breezy a tone as she could manage. "I will cover the expenses. In terms of our finances, my son does not know what he's saying."

Martin gave her a look. His gaze slipped briefly to the hem of her ancient cloak. "Of course not."

She curled her toes sharply against the soles of her shoes, cursing herself for not having donned the cloak her brother and sister-in-law had supplied her with… because of her damned pride. And now her pride was smarting for altogether different reasons. "I insist."

He inclined his head. "Very well."

Oh, God.

As soon as his agreement came, she wanted to cast up the contents of her stomach.

What had she done?

All she'd managed was to shift the responsibility from him to her family.

"That is, unless…"

"Unless?" She pounced, her heart leaping with hope.

"Unless you, as their mother, feel it might be more beneficial for them to clean the mess they've made in the hall."

"Yes," she said so quickly her voice emerged as a garbled croak.

He inclined his head. "I consider that fair."

She managed a nod, even as she knew, and she knew that he knew, there was nothing fair in that offer. Christina should have provided not only the funds to compensate him for the damaged property, but also the workers to clean up the mess.

But he'd offered her a lifeline, one she suspected was born of pity. This time, however, she'd not let her pride again prevent her from accepting an offered lifeline, one that prevented her from needing to go to her family to request the funds. It also saved Christina from offering up further evidence to her family of her children's disastrous manners.

Unable to meet his eyes, she directed her focus to her children as they alternately bickered and gathered their things. "Th-they're usually better behaved than this," she said, lying through her chattering teeth.

"I'm... sure they are. They seem like... perfectly... lovely children."

Mr. Phippen's response came delayed and triply halting.

They had been.

With her husband's illness, everything had changed, and then after his passing, it had changed all the more, and in none of the ways that were for the better.

Still, they were her children. It was one thing to know one's children were vexing. It was an entirely different thing to hear another person say so.

Particularly a tall bear of a man like the stranger before her.

She added a touch of steel to her spine, a lesson she'd learned while a governess had knocked a wooden cane against her back. "I'll have you know, they are—"

"Look, Mama."

She and Martin looked as one over at Luna.

"I'm practicing my throw." The little girl hurled her bonnet.

With reflexes to rival their mouser cat, Martin Phippen shot an arm out, catching the projectile in his capable hand.

Are not, she silently finished the addendum. *They are not lovely.*

She loved them. But they were not well-behaved children. Those were altogether different. She wasn't so blind to their faults and her own as a mother that she wasn't able to recognize that.

"Thank you," she said, swiftly plucking the hat from his fingers. "Now, I bid you good day, Mr. Phippen. Please, let me know when you'd like us to return—"

"Yay," Luna cried. "We're going to come back and break the rest of his windows!"

Rushing over, Christina set Luna's too-big bonnet on her head and then took her daughter by one hand and grabbed for Logan's palm. "You're doing no such thing." Her voice came slightly high pitched to her own ears. "You're returning to clean the mess you've made of Mr. Phippen's properties."

As one, her children groaned.

"But they were alllreaddyy a mess," Lachlan bemoaned.

She looked squarely at her eldest son, who'd become the most unbearable of her brood. "They still belong to him and aren't yours to destroy further."

From the corner of her eye, she caught Mr. Phippen's wry grin. "Why, thank you for that, Mrs. Thacker," he drawled, the roughened hint of East London on his tongue.

He was fascinating and different from anyone she'd personally known in her life.

Christina felt another blush form on her cheeks. It was an odd detail to find herself focusing on, rather than the fact that she'd accidentally insulted the same man whom her children had made a target of their mischief. "Uh, yes... As I was saying, we'll return tomorrow at dawn—"

"Tomorrow at nine."

Her stomach dropped. "Nine o'clock?" At that hour, her family and their guests would all be awake and breaking their fasts, ready to take part in whatever activities her sister and brother-in-law had planned for the day. And she'd have to come up with some excuse as to—

Martin's brow dipped. "Unless there's a problem with that time? Or... if you'd rather just forget the windows all togeth—"

"No!" Her children had wreaked havoc on his home. The condition it had been in was neither here nor there. She'd not raised, and would not raise, children to have a blatant disregard of other people's properties. "It is no problem at all." She took a slow breath. "Lachlan, Logan, and Luna will be here at nine o'clock exactly and see to the damage they did." As it was, he'd already proven far more generous than she or her children deserved. "We will see you at that time, Mr. Phippen." She glanced down at her shockingly silent children. "Make your bows and curtsies."

The moment the order left her, she wanted to call it back and edit for clarity.

Except, it was too late.

Sniggering, her sons dipped a curtsy, while Luna

sketched a bow.

Did she detect the ghost of a grin on Mr. Phippen's lips? She focused her eyes on that hard mouth.

Why… yes, she did.

And strangely, the sight of it did the oddest of things to her heart's rhythm.

Embarrassment. It was just that. Only, that fluttering didn't feel like—

"Good day, Mr. Phippen," she said.

He forsook a bow for a touch of the brim on his hat instead. "Ma'am."

Oddly, she found herself preferring that directness to the fawning of Polite Society.

Unnerved by those thoughts, she caught Luna once more by the hand and urged her children along, tripping slightly at the pace she'd set for them.

"Why are we running?" Luna asked.

"W-we aren't," Christina said, the speed at which she walked and the cold of the day making her breath uneven.

"It feels like a run."

"It's only because your legs are small," Lachlan muttered from behind them.

Luna paused to look back at her brother and stuck her tongue out.

Squeezing her daughter's fingers lightly, Christina directed the girl's focus forward.

"Mr. Phipp is watching us."

"Mr. Phippen," Christina corrected. Despite herself, despite the need for restraint, she found herself edging a discreet look over her shoulder.

He was.

Even ten paces away, the intensity of that steely stare reached.

"*See-ee-ee?*" Luna said, adding several extra syllables in her emphasis.

Christina made herself look away, training her eyes on the path toward her sister's properties. "He's likely making sure we don't come to any harm," she said.

"He's probably making sure we're leaving because he's worried we'll ruin the remaining windows that aren't broken." Lachlan laughed.

Christina gave her eldest son a sharp look. "Hush. We aren't rude, and we aren't disrespectful."

With none of Christina's discreetness, Logan glanced back. His freckle brow furrowed. "No, he's not. He's staring at Mama."

She missed a step and righted herself. "He is watching after all of us," she said with another stolen peek back.

Except…

His eyes are on me…

Catching her notice, Mr. Phippen touched his hat a second time.

Whipping her attention ahead, she moved her children along. "Mr. Phippen was far more generous than you"—*and we*—"deserved. I expect you to be on your best behavior for the remainder of the day, and if you are not, then tomorrow, when you see to the broken windows, I'll also offer him your services cleaning additional parts of his household."

Just like that, her children's keen interest in Mr. Phippen's interest in Christina died. They released matching groans.

"None of that now," she chided, and as she launched into a lecture on proper behavior and her expectations for them, she felt Mr. Phippen's eyes upon her, following her retreat.

And she was grateful with every step that put some distance between her and the handsome stranger who'd managed to disarm her.

Chapter 4

For most of his adult life, Martin hadn't left London, and for that matter, he'd never thought he would. All that had changed as he'd started taking on more and more commissions.

Born to a bricklayer in some of the poorest streets of East London, he'd always felt the expectation that he'd follow in the steps of his late father. Because that's what sons in East London did. That was, if they didn't find themselves succumbing to drink or being seduced by the gang leaders who dwelled in those parts, preying on desperate men, dreaming of a way out—an easy way out.

That, however, hadn't been the case for Martin.

He'd not foreseen his way out of London, but neither had he seen himself aged, and bent, and withered the way his father had been from the brutal work he'd done.

Nay, instead he'd aspired for more. Not the fancy, fine life of the lords and ladies whom he'd eventually found himself working for through the years.

Rather, he'd wanted to own his own business. He'd wanted to not be the hired bricklayer his father was or the builder, but rather, he'd wanted to be the *master* builder, the one overseeing it all. He'd wanted to be the man who employed men—and children—and treated them fairly. And provide himself with a respectable living.

He'd come to appreciate that, regardless of where he lived in London, Town was bustling with people and activity. There was no shortage of adventure. The good sort... and the bad.

He had, however, despite his thoughts on the contrary, left London.

His business had grown and flourished beyond even the greatest expectations he'd had for himself.

His work for noblemen had seen Martin rehabilitating not only their London townhouses, but those same high-paying clients' properties all over the English countryside. The work had taken him into Scotland and Ireland and Wales.

Why, he'd even had one powerful, richer-than-God earl pay Martin to visit France to study a property there so that he could replicate the design layout.

He'd come to appreciate that cities bustled, while the country remained sleepy. There was none of the excitement or chaos to be found in all parts of the big city.

That was, until today.

Having kept some distance between him and his morning visitors, Martin stopped on the fringe of the properties bordering his until he verified that the quartet had found their way safely home.

Squinting, he lifted a hand to his brow, homing in on the young woman and her three children, now mere specks on the horizon, as they made the climb of the stone steps, and then the front doors opened, and Mrs. Thacker motioned for her children to enter. Instead of immediately following, she hovered there and did a long sweep of the snow-covered grounds. Her gaze landed on the tree he stood beside, and she paused for another moment before ultimately disappearing within the manor.

Any other time, he would have been first and foremost fixed on those fascinating properties bordering his. A stone structure more of a keep or castle than country property, it was the manner of interesting to catch any builder's eye, and yet...

His gaze lingered on the last place the young woman had stood, peering back at him.

As if she'd known he was there.

Martin gave his head a shake.

Yes, this was the most eventful morning he'd ever known in the English countryside.

The proud lady and her noisy, troublesome brood were nothing short of lively.

He'd have expected her to balk at the prospect of bringing her children back to clean.

Hell, a lady like her would have, and should have, shunned the offer outright.

The demanding ladies he'd worked for certainly would have not only been horrified at the prospect of their children doing anything so common as clean, but would have also made no offer to compensate him for those injuries to his properties.

Such was the privilege of the ruling elite.

They didn't get that money mattered to most, that it was the stuff that men and women desperately needed to survive.

But Mrs. Thacker knew something about needing money.

That much had been clear in the state of her garments, which had fit not at all with the condition of her sprawling property.

At last relinquishing his place at the border of their estates, he turned and made the long, slow trudge through the snow back to his newly purchased residence.

The moment he entered the freezing-cold household, he doffed his hat, but kept his coat on.

"Brother! You made it!"

"I made it?" He grinned. "I was here last night. It was your arrival that seemed doubtful." With that ribbing that had always been common between them, he folded his younger brother, shorter by an inch and just as broad, in for a big hug.

They patted each other on the back.

"Magnificent, is it not?" his brother marveled the moment they separated.

It took a moment to register what his brother was saying.

Not for the first time, Martin glanced dubiously about, searching for a hint of what exactly his brother was seeing. Perusing, in daylight, the cracked marble floor of the foyer and the water-stained stairs. Surely he'd missed something that his brother saw.

Just then, a lone shard of glass that had retained its place in the panel on the intersecting hall fell, the *plink* of glass echoing in the absolute silence of the servantless, empty house.

His brother leaned around to investigate that sound and,

with a frown, wandered over to the mess of broken windows that had been made by Mrs. Thacker's children. "I'll confess, the last time I came, the windows hadn't been broken. That is, not these windows." He scratched at his brow. "Or I didn't think they were?"

Martin joined Thad. "They weren't," he muttered. "We had company."

At that, his brother, perpetually possessed of a smile, managed to find a frown. "Company?"

Martin briefly filled him in on the details about his morning wake-up greeting from Mrs. Thacker's children, and his mind wandered to his meeting with the delectable beauty herself.

She was taller than most women and possessed of a narrower waist and sharper hips than was his usual preference, yet he'd found himself oddly—

"Ah, we always enjoyed a good window breaking now and then," his brother said, slashing into those improper musings about the young widow.

Martin stared at his brother like he'd gone mad. "A good window breaking. We removed them as part of the work we did for Wingate."

"True," his youngest sibling allowed. "But you're allowing yourself a revisionist version of just how we cleared all those windowpanes. How we'd show up at the work sites after hours so we could finish our task. We'd throw rocks and bricks through them and then clean the mess."

Yes, that much was true.

"This was different," he muttered. "We were seeing to our assignment. These hoydens were destroying property."

"Fair enough." Thad paused. "But surely you see the appeal that drove them to it."

Martin gave his head a wry shake. "You are hopeless."

"I am." Thad grinned broadly. "A hopeless optimist."

That was *also* true. It was a trait that not even his time away serving in the king's army had been able to erase. Thad's ability to grin and jest and tell a grand tale had never left the younger man, and Martin was grateful that his brother remained the way he'd always been.

"And do we know the identity of our visitors?"

"I know they're terrifying," Martin muttered. "The lot of them." He deliberately omitted any specific mention of the young mother who'd also paid a *visit*. "They'll return tomorrow." As his brother wrinkled his brow, he clarified, "They're going to see to the mess they made."

His brother stilled, and then, tossing back his head, he roared his laughter into the high ceiling.

Several birds that had taken shelter in the household were startled into flight, frantically flapping and flying off to another room.

They had birds.

Splendid.

"And what's so amusing about that?" he asked indignantly.

"Only you, my taskmaster of a brother, who is always and only working, would think to have children come and work." Thad shook his head bemusedly. "Now, come," his brother said, thumping him on the back. "Let me show you around the household."

As proud as any owner whose finest cottages and estates

Martin had worked on, his brother beamed and led them off on a tour of the sorry property.

With daylight creeping through the windows and with each step Martin and his brother took to evaluate each room, he realized the depth and breadth of the work this household would require. He'd be bleeding funds to pay for the restoration of the place.

Having grown up and lived a life as poor as everyone else in East London, he'd an appreciation for every shilling and didn't like throwing money away.

They reached the long corridor lined with windows that Lachlan, Luna, and Logan's target practice had taken out, and Martin and his brother stopped.

Nay, there could be no doubting that taking this project on would see him hemorrhage money, and any other time, that would have been his sole focus—this nightmare of an *investment*.

And yet, staring through the windowpaneless windows at the speck of the neighboring property in the distance, he found his mind unwittingly and dangerously tugging back to the proud young mother who'd marched onto his lands that day.

Chapter 5

Christina had always been a dreamer and a wisher, and a believer in miracles.

Her mother had lamented those qualities possessed by her daughter.

Her brother had ofttimes praised her cheery way of being.

Even when her husband had taken ill suddenly with a sickness that had proven debilitating and painful, Christina had clung to her belief in hope.

Until the fortnight prior to his passing, when the pain had been most agonizing, and he'd ceased to open his eyes and see her or their children and had instead been capable only of sleeping and the occasional plaintive moan and whimper. Those devastating sounds had lingered after he'd gone, and they'd made leaving that place where she'd once been happy not so difficult a task.

After that, she'd ceased to believe in all miracles, the big and the small. Any of them.

That was, until yesterday.

Yesterday, after her and her children's return from Mr. Phippen's properties, had proven the first miraculous day Christina had known.

Not only had she managed to return, escaping detection and questions, not one, not two, but three of her free-talking children had said nothing about their meeting with Claire and Caleb's surly at first and far more generous and kinder than they'd deserved neighbor.

With the household awake, and those same three troublesome children bundled up and in tow, Christina should have trusted that the moment of miracles proved transient.

"Where do you think you're going?"

Oh, blast damn and double damn.

Claire's butler, with his fingers on the door handle, held Christina's eye, and with a nearly imperceptible nod and a waggle of his fingers on that same handle, he made his offer clear—he'd yank that panel open and allow her to make a run for it if she wished to pretend she hadn't heard the dowager baroness.

Christina was more than half tempted. If she hadn't already known that this exchange was inevitable.

Alas…

Tamping down a sigh, Christina turned and glanced up at the landing above. "Mother," she said as the silver-haired lady swept slowly down the stone stairs.

Her approach was unhurried, the speed and grace of her steps more befitting a presentation before the queen at court than an older woman greeting her grandbabes, but then, that was how the Dowager Baroness of Bolingbroke always carried herself. Like she was a queen and not the ruthless woman who might or might not have had her hand in the disappearance of the previous Earl of Maxwell. The title had ultimately reverted to its rightful owner, and the crime involved had been subsequently blamed upon Christina's father.

At last, the dowager baroness reached them.

She slid that cold, emotionless gaze over her grandchildren.

The papers had recently resurrected details about the dowager baroness, damning ones that indicated the heartless woman had orchestrated the most heinous of crimes years earlier. Everyone in society knew Christina's father had had a hand in disposing of a young earl when he'd been ill so that he might trade the title of baron for the distant relation's more prestigious, more financially prosperous earldom. Alas, the boy and rightful heir had lived, and the stories surrounding Christina's mother's involvement had recently begun to circulate.

Christina didn't doubt the claims about the ice-cold woman's role in the Earl of Maxwell's disappearance. There was nothing her heartless and unfeeling mother wouldn't do in the name of power and wealth.

"Grandmother," Luna whispered, and hers weren't the excited tones of a child seeing a doting grandparent, but rather, fearful ones.

"Shh," Lachlan whispered, and the little girl instantly complied.

Nothing managed to silence Christina's children like the sight of the dowager baroness. The trio fell into a perfect line and dropped their gazes to the floor.

Why, even the butler edged away, disappearing into the shadows.

Lucky man.

Christina frowned. Her children were hoydens and terribly misbehaved, but she despised it when they became cowed and afraid. And she hated even more that it was her mother, their grandmother, who was responsible for that fear.

"Is there something you need, Mother?" Christina asked, all out of patience.

At her side, each of her children went round-eyed.

The dowager baroness' lips twitched downward at the corners in a disapproving frown. "What do I *need*? I do not need anything. What I want is to know where precisely you are going."

And there it was.

The question she'd desperately sought to avoid being asked.

Her mouth went dry, and she reverted in an instant to the young girl of her childhood who'd been discovered reading books of fairy tales her brother, Tristan, had gifted her.

A small, gloved hand slid into hers, and she looked down.

Luna stared lovingly up, and Christina found her footing.

For she was not a girl. She was a grown woman, with children of her own.

"Did you hear me, Christina? I asked—"

"We are going out to play in the snow."

A gasp issued from her mother's lips, a slight, still-measured exhalation that she gracefully caught behind her fingers. That break in her composure proved short.

The dowager baroness' eyes formed tiny, pinprick slits.

"You are a grown woman, Christina. You do not *play* in the snow." The dowager baroness spared her first glance for her grandchildren. "And it is improper for your children to do so. I should ask you to think of the lesson you are extolling."

The lesson she was *extolling*?

At this point in her life, with everything such a mess, she wasn't sure she was extolling anything of any value that was in any way resonating with her wild children. What she did, however, know was that she'd not have them shamed for playing.

For breaking the windows of a stranger's property? Absolutely, yes.

But even so, it wasn't her mother's place to reprimand them.

Beside her, her three eldest cowered.

"They are children, Mother," Christina said quietly but firmly.

"I'll not debate that point with you. Allow a servant to play with them. You, however, are needed here, Christina. There are guests here."

Ah, yes. That was, of course, the concern and what this cornering was about.

"And you have but a short time to secure a husb—"

Christina gripped her mother's arm and steered the squawking woman off several steps.

"My goodness. *Christina!* Whatever are you doing?" her mother said with a gasp.

Christina steered them to a stop, placing herself between her mother and her children, whose stares had become rabidly curious.

"What do you think you are doing?" Christina demanded in a furious whisper, speaking low enough to keep her children, who were visibly straining to hear, from doing just that.

"What am I doing?" Her mother bristled. "You're the one who is handling me and shoving me about."

Ignoring that misplaced indignation, Christina dropped her voice a fraction. "I'll not have you mentioning a... a..."

"Husband?" her mother supplied.

Christina managed a nod. "That, in front of my children." She paused. "Or, for that matter, in front of anybody."

"But everyone knows that this is the purpose of the party, Christina. And it is time you remember that yourself. You need security, but more importantly, those children behind you need it, as well. The husband you had sure enough did not take care of you."

She gasped. "How dare you?"

"How dare I speak the truth?" her mother shot back. "Easily." Breathing in slowly through her flared nostrils, the dowager baroness calmed herself, before speaking again. "I know you do not wish to be a burden upon your brother and his wife, or your sisters and their husbands."

And yet, that was what she'd become.

Christina balled her hands tight at her sides.

Oh, her siblings and their spouses would never deny her help, and they'd only ever support her, but that did not change the fact that Christina, widowed with four babes and barely a pence to her name, was, in fact, a burden.

"I see that you have come to your senses," her mother

remarked, patting her perfectly elegant coiffure. "Now, see to…" With that same hand that had smoothed her flawless hair, she gestured to Christina's children. "Whatever this is for the day. But when you return, remember that your sole focus this next week must be about finding a husband."

A muscle spasmed at the corner of Christina's right eye, an aggravating tick. "Are we done here?"

Her mother inclined her head. "We are."

Whirling on her heel, Christina marched off.

Claire's butler was immediately there, drawing the panel open for her to sweep outside with her children following close at her heels.

"Come along," she said tightly, not even looking back to see if they followed, knowing they did by the uneven cadence of the crunch of the snow beneath their varying sizes of boots.

Marching back toward Mr. Phippen's, she moved with a like speed she had yesterday when she'd been rushing to retreat from the powerful, quixotic stranger. Only this time, she was racing away from her home and family to him.

She'd known him just a day, but he was safer as a stranger than the words dropped by her mother and the responsibilities bearing down on her.

"Why are we running?" Luna asked, out of breath, and Christina finally slowed.

"We're not."

"We *were*," Lachlan pointed out.

Yes, they had been.

"Because we're running away from Grandmother," Logan said. Her second-eldest son stole a look back toward

Claire's properties. Worry deepened his heavily freckled brow. "I think we need to keep going in case she changes her mind and comes for us."

Yes, she did, too.

"Don't be silly," she said instead, trudging on ahead. "And I'm not afraid of your grandmother," she felt inclined to point out.

At the uncharacteristic and alarming silence from her trio, she looked over.

Each of her children present stared back with like disbelief in their eyes.

"What? I'm not."

"Yes, you are," Lachlan said, flat out rejecting her denial.

Luna gave a big nod that sent her untied bonnet falling into the snow. "He's right. You are."

Christina stopped, pausing to retrieve the bonnet Claire and Caleb had brought back for her during their time in Paris.

She stared at the bright, colorful, sky-blue ribbons, trailing a gloved finger along one of those costly scraps.

A small hand touched her shoulder, pulling Christina from her own musings about her circumstances. "Don't be embarrassed, Mama," Logan said with a maturity she'd not believed any of her children were capable of at this point. "Everyone is afraid of Grandmother."

Grateful he'd misunderstood the reason for her silence, she gave him a thankful smile.

Christina returned the bonnet to Luna's head and tied the ribbons under her daughter's chin into a neat little bow. "She is pretty terrifying, isn't she?" she whispered, giving the ends a little yank.

Luna giggled. "The mostest terrifying of *anyone*."

And though Christina didn't say as much aloud, her daughter was correct on that score.

Straightening, Christina looked off to the stone household in the distance, where Mr. Phippen expected them. "Come along."

When she resumed walking, she set a slower cadence, an easier one for Luna's and Logan's shorter legs.

They arrived a short while later, stopping at the place where they'd last spoken with Mr. Phippen.

Silence hung heavy on the winter landscape, with the steady wind howling forlornly in the sky and the crunch of snow under Luna's boots as she shifted back and forth.

Lifting a hand to her brow, Christina did a small turnabout, searching the area. Only that thick quiet greeted them. It was as though she and her children had collectively imagined anyone's presence yesterday. The snow, disturbed as it had been from their visit yesterday, still containing the imprints of her and her children's feet, along with the larger ones of Mr. Phippen, confirmed the exchange that had played out on these grounds.

"He's not here," she said, her breath leaving a cloud of white in the air.

"Maybe he died," Logan suggested, as casual as if he spoke of the gentleman going off for a horse ride.

"Oh, I hope he didn't," Luna bemoaned. "I like him."

Surprise brought Christina's gaze whipping over to her daughter.

Lachlan looked at her as if she'd lost her mind. "You like

him? He's making us work and yelled at us for breaking his windows."

Luna shrugged. "Well, I do. We were wrong to break his wind—" Her brother shot an elbow into her arm. "Ow. Don't hit me."

"Don't hit your sister," Christina repeated that order and looked to Luna. "You... like Mr. Phippen?"

"I do. He picked you up and made sure you weren't dead, and he could have yelled at us more than he did." Luna chewed at the frayed tip of her glove. "We did break his house, and—" Luna's words abruptly ended, and she looked past Christina's shoulder. Her blue eyes brightened. "He's here!"

As one, Christina, Lachlan, and Logan turned. Marching forth like a veritable Zeus laying seize to the land of the mortals, he moved with such a grace and command. Not even the deep snow could slow his strides.

The breath stuck in her chest and lodged there.

She'd no wish to notice the breadth and power of his form, or the harsh square line of his jaw, or—

"You're late," he said bluntly the moment he reached Christina and her children.

You're late.

Well, if there was a greeting to bring a woman crashing firmly back to reality where the stone-faced fellow was concerned...

Grimacing, thoroughly vexed with herself for noticing him as a man, she gave her head a shake.

"Are you going to dock us payment, Mr. Phippen?" she drawled.

An endearing blush blazed in the gentleman's cheeks, a boylike flush unexpected for a man of his size and strength and command. And it… softened him. In a wonderful way. In a way that made him seem real and reachable.

She startled. Not that she wanted to reach him.

She didn't.

"It was more an observation," he said gruffly. "I didn't think you were coming."

"We were delayed." To give her fingers a task, she tugged off her gloves. "However, I gave my word, Mr. Phippen, and I'm nothing if not a woman of my word."

∽

Martin had awakened this morning expecting he *should* feel annoyed at having to entertain not only a prickly lady, but her three precocious children.

And yet, he'd arisen as he always did at the four o'clock hour, finding himself wide awake… and eager for her return. All four of them.

Given the way he lived his life—for his work, with any relationships outside his familial ones solely revolving around business—it had been a startling discovery.

No, there'd been no way to deny it—he'd been excited about their visit.

It was something he couldn't explain and hadn't wanted to even try… to himself and certainly not to his youngest brother. It was also why he'd been relieved that his brother had arisen at that same early-morn hour and stated his intentions to head to the village to secure a handful of men, women, and children to help make the household habitable while they resided there.

With the passing minutes, however, it had begun to seem like Mrs. Thacker wouldn't show.

And yet, she had.

She was a woman of her word.

The lady pulled off her gloves and stuffed them into the front pocket of her cloak. "I trust you've already planned out our responsibilities for the day, Mr. Phippen? If you can lead the way so we might begin?" Her regal tones befitted a queen, and yet, a lady of the peerage didn't go about asking where she might clean.

"You intend to help?" he asked incredulously.

She winged a dark eyebrow. "You find it so hard to believe that I'll help make amends for my children's misbehaving?"

"Yes," he said flatly. "You're a lady."

"She's only really a Mrs.," the little girl, Luna, chimed in. "Papa was only a merchant, and so none of us are ladies or lords."

Martin moved his gaze quickly over the young mother. Garments or titles aside, Christina Thacker was a lady in all the ways that mattered. He still didn't believe for one moment the lady intended to see this through. She'd shown up, however, which was already a good deal more than he'd credited.

He nudged his chin toward his newly purchased properties. "This way."

Keeping his strides short to accommodate the little ones, Martin led the way.

They reached the front double doors, and he drew one of them open.

Martin motioned them on ahead.

Christina fell back, waiting until her children had filed in, but then hesitated before entering. Her gaze went to the three brooms he'd managed to find in the kitchens and the ash bins, the cleaning supplies neatly lined up against the wall.

This was the moment she'd leave, and it would be better that way for the both of them.

He had work to do.

And she didn't belong in this crumbling keep—

But then the lady marched for the brooms. Collecting the smallest, she motioned for the little girl. "Luna."

Skipping over, Luna took the broom with the same enthusiasm she might a peppermint stick. And then, yanking up her skirts, the girl hopped aboard and proceeded to race around the foyer, cackling perfectly like a witch.

"Logan?" the young widow urged as she collected another broom.

His gaze to the floor and his shoulders bent, the small boy stepped around his sister, still flying herself about the foyer, to take his cleaning equipment for the morning.

Gathering the last broom, Mrs. Thacker held it out for the oldest boy.

Lachlan stood with a mutinous set to his jaw. His arms folded at his chest, he ignored his mother's silent urging.

Mrs. Thacker shook the broom once.

"Lachlan." There was a stern warning in the lady's voice that she neatly layered into the boy's name.

Muttering under his breath, Lachlan dropped his arms to his sides, and stomping over, he snatched the article from his mother's fingers.

All the supplies distributed, Mrs. Thacker looked to Martin.

"Well?"

Well?

The lady sighed. "You are short a broom, Mr. Phippen."

Short a broom?

He glanced about the foyer. Luna continued to fly herself about like some witch of old, while the pair of boys stood side by side, glaring at Martin.

And then it occurred to him.

"You're thinking to clean?" he asked incredulously.

The lady bristled. "And you find that so hard to believe?"

Actually, he did.

His dealings with women were… few. The simple reason being his work consumed him and didn't allow for anything beyond the occasional physical gratification. But he'd worked long enough for and with the peerage to know their women didn't show up to clean houses, and he found an unexpected appreciation stir within him for the young mother.

"I appreciate that, ma'am, but you didn't make the mess. These three did, and as such, you shouldn't be cleaning up after them."

Fire flashed in her eyes.

At his rejection? Or because he'd interjected on parenting matters?

Based on the wealth of pride this one possessed, he'd

wager firmly on the latter.

"Be that as it may, Mr. Phippen, I would—"

"It's our job, Mama," Logan interjected, interrupting the spirited woman's challenge. "We did it, and we don't need you to clean after us."

Lachlan glared sharply at his younger brother, but Logan ignored the looks being cast his way.

In that moment, the youngest boy grew in Martin's estimation.

"If you'll follow me," Martin said and motioned to the trio of children.

Lachlan flipped his broom so the head with the bristles rested against his shoulder. Logan hurried to imitate the actions of his brother so he was a smaller, shorter image of the taller boy.

They fell into a slow, reluctant step, trailing after Martin.

Luna immediately altered course and directed her flying broom in the direction he'd indicated, periodically cutting across, back and forth, as if she were flying ahead of him.

Luna laughed like an old crone in a high, pretend aged voice. "Hee-hee-hee."

All the while, Mrs. Thacker followed closely after them.

Suddenly, Luna tossed a glance back. "Look, Lachlan," the girl called. "I am Grandmother." With that, she released another perfect witch's cackle.

The two boys sniggered loudly, nearly drowning out their mother's gasp. Nearly.

Martin's ears pricked up.

A blush splotched the lady's cheeks, and her startled gaze flew to Martin and then back to her daughter. "Luna," she said sharply.

The little girl, however, gave no indication she either heard or cared, instead continuing on in her witch's voice until Martin brought them to a stop at the door to one of the parlors.

After they'd assembled in the room, he motioned to the glass covering the floor. "Sweep the glass into piles. Don't go picking the remnants up, or you might get yourselves cut."

It was a worry he didn't have with the boys and girls in London he employed. Those children were familiar with work and had been employed in crumbling properties often enough to conduct themselves like seasoned builders.

Mrs. Thacker's children, however, were not skilled in those same ways, and as such, he'd not see them hurt.

Logan had flipped his broom over to begin sweeping when his elder brother shot a hand up, silently ordering him to stop.

Lachlan glared darkly at Martin. "Do you think we're babes, hmm? That we don't know how to clean up glass?"

"Lachlan," Mrs. Thacker said warningly.

Martin lifted a hand, holding off that scolding.

Tension crackled in the room.

The boy was angry.

Palpable rage oozed from every corner of his small frame.

He'd known many boys like the one before him. He'd employed any number of them over the years... and he'd been one himself.

Until the successful builder he'd been hired to do work for had taken him under his wing and given Martin a new view of what his future could be. That man had changed the course of Martin's life. Since then, Martin never failed to detect the pent-up frustration of children who wished their lives were something different than they were.

"I think it's safer that you don't pick up the glass, and as a builder, I know a thing about ensuring the safety of those working for me."

Lachlan jabbed his broom at Martin. "I don't *work* for you."

"In this moment, you do."

Brimming with anger, the boy glowered at Martin. Martin, however, returned that stare with only a quiet calm.

Muttering to himself, Lachlan put his broom to the floor and set to sweeping.

"Will you show me the rest?" That quiet, thin query brought Martin's attention over to Mrs. Thacker.

He gave her a questioning look, and she clarified. "The rest of… what they did to your household."

"There's no reason for—"

"There is every reason for it, Mr. Phippen," she cut in, her tones no-nonsense. "I am their mother, and I would see the extent of the damage they are responsible for." The fiery glimmer in her pretty eyes dared him to defy her.

Martin knew better than to challenge one with that look. "First, given our recent familiarity, I expect we've moved on to calling one another by our names. I'm Martin."

"I couldn't."

He snorted. "And why not?"

The lady drew back, her lips slipping apart a fraction. "I…"

"Because Grandmother wouldn't allow it," Lachlan

called over and promptly laughed.

A pink blush filled the lady's cheeks as she leaned around Martin and glared at her son. "Enough," she mouthed.

The boy gave no indication he'd heard or cared about that directive.

Martin examined that exchange. Yes, the child was angry. Not only that, but he was also taking those feelings out on his mother. He'd been that child once himself.

Christina glanced back at Martin, and he swiftly slid his eyes away from his earlier study, lest she note that attention. With her pride, she'd only be offended.

"Lachlan," Martin called over in the firm, quiet way he reserved for some of his more hotheaded employees.

The child flushed, but almost instantly returned to the task he'd been assigned.

"Very well, Martin," she said, with a slight emphasis upon his name, though the whisper was a testament to the fact that she sought to conceal that informality from her children. "You may call me Christina."

Christina.

It was an uncharacteristic name for an English lady, as uncommon as the proud woman herself.

"Christina, you don't need to see the rest of… the state of the house," he said, returning to her earlier request.

That upside-down mouth of hers—full upper lip, intriguingly thinner lower—grew taut. "You don't need to tell me what I need or do not need, Martin. I'm their mother. Furthermore, I'm not looking for you to protect me from their actions. I'd know the full extent of what they've done here, and in all matters in general."

Which already made her an oddity among the previous ladies he'd knowledge of.

How many former clients either hadn't known or cared that their hellions had been underfoot, wreaking havoc on a project?

"Well?" she demanded, mistaking the reason for his protracted silence.

He inclined his head. "Fair enough. Follow me." Martin led her from the room and through the window-filled corridors, most of which were now bare of any panes.

As they went, the gaze Christina moved over the damage grew more and more stricken, and he immediately wished he'd denied her request, because seeing her this way caused an odd squeezing sensation in his chest.

She lingered her stare upon a smattering of crystal that lay like a frozen icicle that had been shattered into a thousand tiny fragments. "My goodness," she whispered.

"The panes were all going to have to be replaced anyway." Nor was his just a false assurance.

Lifting her eyes, she looked at him. "You are being generous, Martin," she said, her voice sad.

He snorted. "I'm not. It just moved up the timing of when this particular part of the project would have to be seen to."

"Show me the rest."

"There's nothing more to see," he insisted. "They—"

Her fingers came up, touching his sleeve, and a jolt went through him, a spark as powerful as the charge just before a lightning strike.

The shock of that warmth froze him, and he stared at her

long fingers upon him.

"I don't want you to protect me from what my children did," she said softly. "I want to know."

And he found his appreciation for her doubling that day.

His gaze slipped once more to her fingers upon his coat sleeve, and then she curled them briefly upon him before suddenly yanking her palm back, as if she'd been burned.

Resuming the tour, he paused periodically to reveal another room that bore her children's handiwork.

"They really did make a mess." So much horror and shame and sadness filled those quietly whispered words that he looked over.

"It's fine."

"It's not," she said instantly. "It's not fine. I don't... even know who they *are* anymore." That admission exploded from her lips on a hushed whisper. "My children. They are rude and boorish and misbehaved, and they weren't that way." All her words rolled and tumbled together, and her chest moved quickly, her breath coming in slight gasping heaves. "They used to be polite and good and kind. They would have never done"—she waved a hand around the room—"this. And the thing of it is..." Christina wrapped her arms around her middle. "I don't even know when it happened. He was so sick. So very sick, and it came on so sudden and took hold of him, and our family became consumed with his illness."

The lady's husband. Somewhere along the way, he'd wager she'd stopped speaking to him and just spoke in general the truthful words she'd been wanting to speak—no, needing to speak.

"I was too busy trying to not collapse and dissolve into nothing, and in the midst of surviving, I lost control of it all."

Her words faded into a barely there whisper, and she stood, hugging herself in a sad, solitary embrace.

"It's new," he said quietly. "You're all going to be looking to find your way again, and that isn't something that just happens, Christina." He joined her and then, brushing his knuckles along her chin, brought her eyes up to his. "But it eventually comes."

As if only recalling his presence, Christina started, her arms falling swiftly to her sides and color blooming on her cheeks. "You don't know anything about it," she said tersely, jerking her jaw from his touch. "So please, you and everyone else should refrain from telling me what I'm experiencing and how I will eventually feel." With that, she started with brisk steps toward the path they'd traveled.

He should let her go.

Let her to her erroneous opinion and leave her and her angry children as he'd found them.

And yet, maybe it was pity, maybe it was remorse, or maybe it was something more he couldn't, and shouldn't, put his finger on, but something about her and her children compelled him in ways he didn't understand.

"Actually, I do know something about it," he called after her.

Christina abruptly stopped, her skirts whipping about her ankles.

She turned, facing him once more. "What?" she asked, the question emerging hesitantly as she rejoined him.

Did the lady even know she'd returned to his side?

"Not in the same way," he quickly added. He'd never had a wife, and with his work and responsibilities, he didn't see himself settling down anytime in the near—or even distant—future.

At the question in her eyes, he clarified. "I'd a sister, a younger sister. She caught scarlet fever. One day, she was playing happily and singing and skipping a doll around our one-room cottage, and the next, her cheeks were flush with fever, and she couldn't manage anything more than a whimper and moan." He scrubbed a hand down the side of his face. "She went quickly. Here one moment, gone the next. With only broken hearts and a heavy quiet left in her absence."

Her lips parted, and she rested a delicate gloved palm upon his arm. "I'm so sorry, Martin."

"Alice was the only sister among three boys and cherished all the more for it by me and our parents. She sang absolutely everything. Greetings. Good mornings." That remembrance of his jovial little sister brought his lips curving up in a wistful smile. "A boy couldn't stay angry at her, even when she did things like steal a handful of toy soldiers and toss them into the Thames to see which one could swim the farthest."

A laugh bubbled past Christina's lips, filtering into the quiet around them, and he found himself laughing in return.

When that gentle amusement faded, he gave his head a sad shake. "Oh, there was a void when she was gone," he said softly into the quiet.

It had been years since he'd talked about her. In the

beginning, that had been because his parents had been bereft at any hint of mention of their beloved daughter. And then because it had been simply easier to… forget.

"I find myself not able to remember the good times." That whisper cut across his musings, and he looked down at the woman before him. "There was so much sadness and pain. That's all I can feel and remember anymore."

Taking her hands in his, he drew them close to his chest and squeezed lightly. "It won't always be that way," he said. "I can promise you that."

Christina caught her lower lip between her teeth, biting that flesh. "Thank you."

His eyes slid down to their linked fingers. He'd no place touching her.

Even he—nay, especially he—a master builder born in East London, knew that.

Reluctantly, he slackened his grip and made to release her, but Christina held on, squeezing him back, lightly, before breaking that connection.

They resumed their stroll, and he opened his mouth to point out that they'd reached the end of the damage that had been wrought by her children and suggest they return…

But she continued on, her enrapt gaze taking in the stone floors of the halls, and given the sadness of before had receded from her gaze, he was reluctant to end her study.

Liar. For whatever reason, you are enjoying her company.

Discomfited by that niggling voice mocking him in his mind, Martin followed after her, leaving a slight distance. A safe distance meant to resurrect the walls that left them as strangers and put a stop to that moment of connection they'd shared... and his admiration for her.

The young woman, however, seemed to have no such similar awareness of Martin. Rather, she took in the brocade needlework, throwbacks to a long-ago time that had since grown faded and tattered. A lady of her elevated station would only be horrified at what she saw, and that was without the mess her children had made.

Suddenly, she slowed her steps before coming to a full stop before an embroidery of an armor-clad man being knighted.

She stroked her fingers with an almost reverence along the trim. "It is beautiful," she whispered, and for a moment, Martin looked about in search of the things of beauty responsible for those awed tones before realizing she'd referred to the hanging.

"What?" he blurted. The faded rag she now lovingly caressed?

Suddenly, Christina released the material from her fingers and did a small circle, stretching her arms out as she did that pirouette. "*All* of this."

He started, and then a laugh rumbled from his chest before he registered the frown puckering her forehead and that place between her eyebrows. Then the truth hit him like the weight of bricks that had once rained down on him as a boy on his first day of bricklaying with his father. "You think *this* is beautiful?"

"I do," she said, not missing a beat.

By the firm disapproval in her tone, she meant it.

He gave his head a rueful shake. "And here I thought my brother, the one swindled into purchasing this heap, was the only one to feel that way about it."

"Then your brother has impeccable taste," she shot back, and damned if he didn't find himself envying that praise she heaped upon his less-than-savvy-in-matters-of-business brother.

"For I don't know what you are seeing, Martin," she went on with a touch of sadness to that pronouncement, and then, with a wistful, faraway gaze, she stared out the still-intact glass panels of the floor-to-ceiling windows lining the hall. "There are traces of the new world blended with that of the old. A perfect mix of what was once here and what could be again," she murmured.

He stared, riveted, transfixed.

Not by his newly inherited property.

Her. I'm seeing her.

The sun had finally begun to find its place upon the early morning sky, that bright orange orb illuminating the world around them, shining through the frost-covered windows, and bathing Christina in the softest, warmest light.

"I don't see it that way," he admitted.

As if she remembered she wasn't alone, the young woman started, touching a hand to her throat and looking back. That pretty blush of before returned to bathe her cream-white cheeks in a soft shade of red.

"And how do you see it, Martin?"

"Like an expensive project that doesn't make sense." Stuffing his hands in his pockets, he nudged his chin to indicate the space around them. "It's crumbling and in sorry disrepair and will cost more money than it'll ever be worth to refurbish. Certainly more than it will ever fetch."

A sad glimmer sparked in her eyes. "That is a sad way of seeing this compelling place, Martin."

Compelling?

He gave the space around them a skeptical look.

As though he were forgotten once more, Christina resumed her walk, trailing slowly ahead, skimming her fingers along the cracked stone pillars lining the corridor, touching the crisscrossed metal bars upon the last glass panels that hadn't surrendered their place from those frames.

As she went, he followed along slowly after her.

Periodically, she paused to peek inside a room, and with each discovery, the wonderment in her expressive gaze grew.

He'd never before known a woman to look upon a structure and its connected lands the way he did. And for the first time since his arrival, he saw the place in a different light. He saw it through her eyes.

Why, she looked at this manor the way he did all properties.

He paused.

Or rather, the way he once had.

When he'd first been hired as an architect and master builder, he'd been hungry, seeing the possibilities in all the properties he passed. It hadn't mattered how dilapidated, how ancient, how much work was required.

He stopped and stared unblinkingly ahead at the tall, Spartan warrioress wandering the halls.

"You're right," he said into the quiet.

Christina's steps slowed, and she cast a questioning glance over her shoulder.

"I... It is." Martin took another look around, seeing it

with new eyes and an appreciation he'd failed to have from the start.

The lady narrowed her eyes. "You're having a laugh at me now," she said tartly and swept past, heading back the way they'd started, but he caught her lightly by the arm, staying her.

"Not at all." He moved his stare over the delicate planes of her face, her pert, delicately pointed nose. "I've been looking at it in terms of costs and expenses, and all that clouded my vision to what it was and... what it could be."

Remembering he still held her, Martin released her. "In fact, I don't even know when I stopped seeing buildings and land the way you do, the way I *used* to..." Hell, he didn't even know when the shift had happened.

It simply had.

Christina drifted closer. Tall as she was, she tipped her head back the merest fraction to meet his eyes, and his breath stuck in his lungs. Her breath, containing the trace scents of honey and chocolate, sweet and delectable, wafted over his skin. And he angled his head lower to meet that kiss she held out.

"When I was a girl..." she said softly, her words unexpected, the kiss he'd craved having been no more than an illusion conjured by his own hungering for her. He froze, as it took a moment for her whisper-soft words to cut through the haze of desire thoroughly befuddling his senses.

"One of my sisters wrote..." A smile formed on her upside-down, full mouth. "Faye penned deliciously wicked stories that horrified my mother when she discovered them one day. My other sister, Claire, painted and was... is quite good at it."

"And you?" he prodded, impatient to know.

"And I wished to design the inside of households. My father had recently inherited an earldom." Her lips twisted in a nearly imperceptible grimace that, had he not been studying her as close as he had, he would have missed, and he wondered at the meaning behind it. "And my parents immediately put their newly inherited resources into improving the households. There were always workers bustling about, and it was garish and gaudy, and every day, I'd steal one of Claire's sketchpads and on those pages create alternate visions of what our home could be."

"And what would your home look like?" he asked, brushing a curl back from her brow and tucking it behind her ear.

Engrossed in her telling, she failed to note his bold touch.

"Pale blue walls," she said, her voice growing more excited as she spoke. "Not the obscenely bright colors favored by so many ladies, but an understated shade the same hue as a summer sky so that for all the many days of English rain and gray skies, there's always something cheerful and warm."

Her eyes as bright as the vision she now painted, Christina gestured with her hands, as if painting the scene before them. And never in all of his life had he known a woman who'd been as lost as he'd been himself in the wonder of imagining something and designing it. His breath hitched, and it was as though he'd run a race, with his heart hammering as he tried to reconfigure a way to get air into his lungs.

"I'd not have extravagant wallpaper in all gold, but rather, highlight the soft beauty of those blues with the faintest trims of gold along the paneling and—" She ceased speaking, another pretty blush blooming in her cheeks. "Are you making light?"

Her hurt-filled query brought his feet crashing back to earth. "Just the opposite. I found myself…" Enrapt. Captivated. Enthralled. "Engrossed in"—*you*—"the vision you painted."

Her thick lashes swept down a sliver more as she continued to assess him in that searching way.

"Why would you think I'm making light of you, Christina?" he asked.

On the heels of that challenge, the suspicion lifted from features that revealed her every emotion. She looked down at her bare hands. "I am… unaccustomed to men who welcome such opinions on such matters."

In other words, the lady's husband hadn't encouraged her to celebrate those passions she clearly possessed. "Your husband didn't support your passion for designing."

"I didn't say that!" she exclaimed, defensiveness mixing with guilt and confirming his supposition.

"You didn't need to." Everything he'd witnessed from most of those stuffy, pompous fellows made them ones who'd keep their women as pretty ornaments and never freely support whatever passions those ladies might possess.

Splotches of furious color marred her cheeks, that crimson color different than the softer blushes of before. "I'll not have you speak ill of my late husband," she said, taking an angry step toward him. "I'll have you know he was a good man and a good husband."

"Whoa," he said, as though handling a temperamental

designer who didn't take to having their visions challenged. "I'm not talking poorly of the fellow."

"I'll have you know, when we were able, he allowed me free rein to design our household as I saw fit."

"But that wouldn't be enough for you," he said before he could keep from speaking that statement aloud. Nor, for that matter, did he want to recall it.

The lady drew back, shock replacing her earlier affront. "You don't know that."

"I do," he said in an instant.

There could be no doubting that Christina had been bit by the same bug that had taken a chomp out of Martin years earlier. "I know passion for design when I see it in a person, because I've had it my whole life." Martin shrugged. "And despite what silly rules and expectations your peerage has for ladies, a love for design is something that men and women both possess, and when you have a desire to create, well, there's no fighting the pull of it."

Her eyes went soft. Her lips slipped apart. "Well," she said, that single syllable a breathy exclamation.

His throat worked several times as—God help him—he found himself noticing all over again her mouth and the tiny brown birthmark dusting the edge of her right nostril, an endearing imperfection upon her skin.

"And..." The word trailed off, and in her eyes, he caught the glimmer of indecision as she battled between asking the question she clearly wished an answer to and honoring whatever Polite Society's rule was on indulging in discussions with strange men.

He remained silent, not prodding her. He'd have her

freely ask for the information she wished to know and have her do that when, and if, she were ready.

"Do you know women who've… done those things? Indulged in those passions?"

"It's not an indulgence to pursue work one loves," he said without inflection. An earl's daughter wouldn't know that. Hell, most earls' daughters wouldn't think to ask questions about it. "And yes, I've taken the assignments of women who own their own businesses and who possess complete control of the vision they have for it."

Her eyes took on a faraway, wistful quality. "My sisters are not unlike that. They are both married, but Claire, she paints and has even visited universities in Europe, and Faye writes articles. Important ones about injustices, exposing those who've wronged others. They are younger than I, but they are like those women you speak of. More than I'll ever be." She spoke that last part as more of a regretful afterthought that clouded her eyes with sadness he wished to chase away.

"And why not?" he shot back.

Chapter 6

Why not? Mr. Martin Phippen, the builder, asked.

He asked to know why she didn't indulge in her... passions, as he'd called them.

A little laugh spilled out, and she shook her head.

A frown formed on his hard lips.

And then it hit Christina. Why... "You're serious," she blurted.

"Deadly," he said. "You enjoy designing interiors, and given the fact you are able to see past the disrepair of this hovel and the ideas you have in terms of color, you clearly have an eye for it."

He was an oddity, this man.

He spoke of women proprietors whom he'd worked for with the same ease he now presented the possibility of her taking on design projects.

Whereas her late husband had been content for her to embroider.

She'd been content.

But were you happy in those endeavors? a voice taunted at the back of her mind. *Were you truly happy darning stockings and knitting blankets and—*

"Because women do not work," she said.

"I just told you they do."

God, he was tenacious.

She gritted her teeth, never having been so challenged. Not by her father, nor her brother, nor her late husband.

"Well, I cannot."

He folded his arms across that broad, barrel-sized chest and winged a dark eyebrow.

Her patience, her one great virtue, as her mother had often backhandedly complimented her for, reached its end. "Because I'm a lady. Because ladies… We aren't permitted those opportunities. Not because some of us do not wish to," she said, lest he assume she was too proud and self-important. "We do not have the funds to do with as we wish. We have to answer to husbands or brothers or fathers."

"Well, that is a lot of shite."

"I don't make the rules, Martin," she said bitterly.

"You just follow them."

He spoke matter-of-factly, and yet, something about that set her teeth on edge.

"Yes, I follow them because women do not have the freedom not to."

"Your sisters sound like they've found themselves bucking convention."

Once again, his was a casual statement, one that praised Faye and Claire—as they deserved—and yet, also served to remind Christina that she'd always been the dutiful daughter, sister, and wife. The vapid, uninteresting one who'd always done precisely as she'd been expected to do, by both her parents and society.

Painfully aware of the heavy silence, she lifted her chin.

"I don't have the same luxuries as my sisters. They have funds, I do not," she said bluntly, speaking of her finances in a way that immediately brought her toes curling in humiliation and in a way that would have sent her mother into a faint. "I have four children who are fatherless, and I'm just trying to survive and sort my way through this bloody mess, and so I do not have the ability to simply indulge in my passions." Those final words echoed and pinged off the high ceilings, and she winced, failing to realize her voice had climbed and carried.

She pressed her hands to her cheeks and drew in a breath. "Forgive me." What was it about this man that had her speaking freely about the most intimate and difficult parts of her life and her situation?

Martin shook his head. "There's no apologies necessary, Christina," he said quietly. "I respect the fact that you have others whose care you're reliant upon." He took a step closer. "I just don't want you to fail to acknowledge what you deserve and want: You enjoy designing interiors. You have vision. You deserve to pursue that if you wish. You deserve to be happy, Christina. Whatever will bring you joy…"

He spoke about what she deserved and what made her happy? When was the last time she, or anyone, had acknowledged what she wished for from life? Once a woman became a mother, her life became inextricably intertwined with the humans she'd brought into this world. The lives of her four young children had become hers. She'd not even realized she'd lost parts of herself until Martin Phippen, a builder whom she'd known just a day, had pointed it out. In fact, she'd not even known she'd been missing those pieces of herself. "I've never thought of it in that way, because I really haven't been able to," she explained, wishing for him to understand. For reasons she didn't understand, it was important for him to know why she wasn't one of those progressive ladies such as the ones he'd worked with and for. Or such as her sisters. "My days are consumed with my children, and I've four of them."

"Four?"

"Lara is just a little over one. And you've already met Lachlan, Logan, and Luna." A pained laugh escaped her. "As such, you can probably gather that finding time for projects I'm passionate about, well, it really isn't feasible."

His lips tipped at the right corner, that crooked smile causing a fluttering down low in her belly, a sensation she'd not known in so very long. But then his grin faded, and that hard line formed once more on his mouth. "Trust me, as someone who was born in East London and worked since the moment I was all but first walking, I know a thing or two about not finding the time."

It was a humbling reminder of the existence he'd lived, one that was honorable, but also one that, by everything he'd revealed in the short time she'd known him, had been harsh and hard and unforgiving.

Martin touched his fingertips to her chin, tipping her gaze up to his.

"But, Christina, the time isn't ever going to be there."

His eyes moved over her face in a way that stole her breath and left her warm inside.

"The time to look after yourself, it's not just going to present itself, for all the reasons you already said. It's about *taking* the time you need." The words he spoke, however, proved even more entrancing. "You're going to be no good to yourself or your children if you aren't feeding your passions and looking after yourself."

She bit her lip. It was the first time since her husband had fallen ill that anyone had urged her to nurture herself. Oh, her siblings and their spouses had been supportive, and they'd even helped as they were able with her precocious children. But no one had encouraged her to find—nay, as Martin had said—*take* any time for her own. "Thank you," she said softly. She didn't know that there would ever be an opportunity for her to live as he'd suggested, but he'd asked after her and put her first, and she would be forever grateful to him for that reason alone.

He nodded and then slowly removed his fingers from her chin, and she missed that touch.

That was something else she'd been so much without.

And she'd not thought about it until this man before her.

"Please, don't," she said quietly, swiftly, knowing there should be a deeper humiliation at that plea.

And yet, she'd missed being touched. Being held.

Passion darkened his eyes, and his hands came up once more. This time, he gripped her narrow waist, his fingers tightening reflexively upon her. Her skin burned hot through the light wool of her fabric.

And Christina didn't retreat. She didn't draw back. Instead, she swayed toward him, her body bending like a bud in a spring breeze, erasing the small space that existed between them.

Hunger went through her, a whisper of need contained

within her body's movements, and he lowered his mouth. Slowly.

He is going to kiss me.

She'd wager her soul. His very gradual descent even now allowed her the time to retreat, and he ceded her ability to either surrender to his embrace or the opportunity to step aside.

And what was worse…

She longed for that kiss.

And what was most terrifying, she longed for *this man's* kiss.

Christina closed her eyes, and her head fall back.

Then he stopped. She felt his breath caress her skin. She heard it coming fast and hard.

Unable to look at him, she let herself be trapped in this moment she shamefully wished to be in. She let her fingers come up, and she curled them about his arms, gripping him, exploring his muscles. She'd never known a man built like him. She'd never known a man *could* be. All sinew and strength. Power and hardness. Like those carved sculptures crafted of marble, but emanating pure heat.

His breathing grew raspier. Or was that her own?

Everything was all mixed up in her mind.

Then he began to lower his mouth again—

"What are you doing?"

Christina came careening right back to earth, pushed into a hard landing by the suspicious tones of her eldest son.

She whirled around to find Lachlan alongside a man nearly as tall, but not nearly as broad, and of the same coloring as Martin.

Mortified heat blazed across Christina's body. "Lachlan," she blurted.

"Yeah. Lachlan." Her son narrowed his eyes and moved his stare between Christina and Martin. "What are you doing?"

Her mind stalled, and she drew an absolute blank.

Fortunately, Martin proved quicker on his feet. "Your mother's necklace had fallen, and I'd just helped her secure it."

Christina's hand shot to the gold chain and the small heart pendant that rested there. She closed her fingers around the piece given to her by her husband years earlier. And guilt, so much guilt, at what she'd been about to do, at what she'd wanted to do, and at her son's almost discovery, washed through her.

She took a quick step away. "I am so grateful to you for your help." More specifically, she was grateful for his quick thinking on the necklace.

That deep glimmer of suspicion in Lachlan dimmed. Perhaps had her son been older, he'd have easily recognized the lie. As it was, there could be no doubting the grown man beside him saw all too well.

The coarsely dressed stranger immediately masked his feelings.

"Mrs. Thacker," Martin said, "allow me to introduce you to my business partner and brother, Mr. Thaddeus Phippen."

His brother?

"It is a pleasure," she said, grateful for the distraction.

"I didn't know your necklace was broken," Lachlan said,

a touch of suspicion remaining in his voice.

She froze. Alas, it appeared she'd underestimated her son's innocence.

A sharp cry rang out, saving her from answering.

Her gaze flew in the direction of that sound, which was immediately followed by great, big, unmistakable wails. Her heart climbed to her throat as, with a gasp, she took off running. "Luna!"

Her steps were overtaken by Martin as he went sprinting past. Gathering up her skirts, Christina quickened her strides and rushed after him, racing toward her daughter. "Luna!" she called again.

She arrived just after Martin and rushed past him to reach her daughter.

Christina skidded to a stop, dropping to the floor and taking her daughter by her small shoulders. She ran her hands searchingly over the sobbing girl. "What is it, sweet?" she pleaded, finding nothing.

"He's dyyyyying!" Luna sobbed.

She followed her daughter's trembling, stretched-out finger over to where Martin knelt alongside Logan.

Christina's gaze went to a small droplet of blood on the ground, and fear filled her throat. "Logan," she rasped, rushing over.

Alas, her son proved far calmer than Christina, as did the gentleman who knelt before him, tenderly wrapping his left hand, murmuring as he did.

She came up short beside the pair.

In all the years she'd been a mother, Christina had tended to many injuries. She'd wrapped many scrapes sustained during play and brushed away many tears cried because of those injuries. Never before, however, had she witnessed a man oversee that tender task.

Growing up, Christina's own father hadn't bothered with her or her siblings. He'd been far too self-important to do so. As such, she'd been more than awed by the fact that her late husband had played with his children and taken an interest in their lives, scolding them when the situation merited it, reading to them every night. Never, however, had her husband cared for her children's scrapes the way this man before her was.

And she stared on, riveted by the ease with which he looked after Logan.

"... shouldn't have done it," Logan was mumbling under his breath, while Martin dusted his white kerchief over her son's palm. "Lachlan said since we were cleaning, we should decide how we did it." Logan paused to shoot a glare in his older brother's direction.

Lachlan blushed, but his mouth was set in stony obstinance.

"Well, regrets won't fix your hand, but they will hopefully help you in the future when making decisions," Martin said with none of the told-you-so tones the moment absolutely merited. He reached inside his jacket and removed a small leather case.

Christina angled her head to examine that article.

"What is that?" Luna's tears had faded to the occasional watery hiccough, and the girl rubbed her little fists over her cheeks.

Martin glanced past Lachlan and over to the girl. "It's

called a nipper. I did work for an inventor once, and he fashioned them for me."

Wide-eyed, both Luna and Logan took a step closer. Even a wary Lachlan edged nearer to study the leather case.

"When I'm overseeing the construction of a building, I've any number of people who work for me working with glass and wood, and it's not uncommon for the occasional scrape to happen." As he spoke, he popped open the case and showed it to Christina's children. Even Christina found herself drawn closer by the curiosity of those unfamiliar tools. "A gentleman whose home I was responsible for the design of observed the handful of occasions when my workers suffered from a piece of glass or wood in their hand and crafted this set for me." He removed a small, slender metal piece and proceeded to demonstrate how the item worked.

Logan recoiled.

"Oh no," Luna whispered. "Does Logan have… a splinter?"

Christina's youngest son immediately drew his hand protectively close to his chest.

"There's several small pieces of glass lodged," Martin said, and Christina's stomach churned.

"Nooooo," Luna wailed and commenced crying again.

"Shh," Christina murmured as her daughter buried her head against her skirts.

Although she could relate. Christina was not squeamish when caring for bloody noses or sprained ankles, or even when the children had the occasional stomach upset that had them casting up their accounts.

But having to remove splinters when they'd been climbing the trees outside or playing in their wood fort had been a task she'd despised above all others.

"I don't want to have it removed," Logan cried, scrambling away from Martin and moving behind Christina. "It'll just come out on its own."

"It's not safe for it to remain in there," Martin said in soothing tones. "It can get infected, and then you'll be worse off."

The other Mr. Phippen stepped forward. "I can assure you, there isn't a finer splinter remover than Martin. Why, he's been plucking glass and slivers of wood and brick from my hands and feet since he was not even seven."

That broke into Luna's blubbering. She went instantly quiet. "Really?" she asked.

Martin's brother nodded. "He sure has. And as he said, he's taken care of any of the men, women, and children who work for him that end up with a sliver."

Logan wavered, indecision keen in his revealing eyes, before he took one step and another closer to Martin, coming to a stop right before him.

Her son hesitated a moment and then thrust his palm toward Martin. "Fine," he muttered. "Do it."

"You don't need him to do it," Lachlan snapped. "Just because he says he's taken out splinters doesn't mean he has. And you know, Mama thinks it's fine to leave them in."

"Yeah, but that's only because Mama hates splinters."

All eyes went to Christina, and her cheeks fired hot under the room's scrutiny.

"I don't... avoid plucking them out," she said, resisting

the urge to squirm.

"Yes, you do," Luna piped in.

"Sometimes it just… seems better to let them be." She saw as much as felt the slight smile ghosting Martin's lips.

"It's really not," the other Mr. Phippen volunteered.

"And you know so much about it, too?" Lachlan rejoined in such a disrespectful challenge that Christina felt another blush form.

"Lachlan," she warned.

Mr. Thad Phippen, however, continued, addressing her anger-filled son. "Actually, I do. I served in the king's army and had any number of experiences watching doctors and other people pluck… splinters from people."

Lachlan rocked back on his heels. "Oh," he said.

"You are a soldier!" Luna cried happily. Quitting Christina's side, the little girl raced over to Martin's brother and grabbed his hand, giving it a hard pull. "You must tell us about it. Please. Pleeease."

"Luna!" Christina entreated. "That isn't polite." She looked to Mr. Thad Phippen. "Forgive me." As it was, her brother, Tristan, had served in the king's army, and the war was not something he wished to ever speak about.

He touched the brim of his hat. "No apologies necessary." The Phippen brothers shared a look. "In fact, if Lachlan and Luna wish to hear more about my time serving in the king's army, I'd be happy to share with them, including some of the things in my rucksack."

Christina understood in a moment the message behind that silent exchange.

"Oh, tell us!" Luna exclaimed, clapping happily.

"I... might be interested in hearing about it," Lachlan said grudgingly.

With a nod, Martin's brother urged them along.

Logan attempted to hurry after them, but Christina placed a staying hand on his shoulder. "Not you, my dear."

Her youngest son groaned.

"He didn't have to do that," Christina said after the three had left, and only she and Martin and Logan remained.

"No, but he'll take care with what he shares with his audience." In other words, he'd not regale them with terrifying tales, but would merely provide a diversion so that Logan could be cared for.

"Well, I want to go, too," Logan pleaded, tugging at Christina's cloak. "I don't need to have the glass taken out. Don't let him take it out. *Please.*"

"I would never do anything that you didn't yourself allow," Martin said, and the solemn, matter-of-fact way in which he spoke to Logan, as though he were a social equal and not a small child, managed to penetrate her son's panicky response.

Her son glanced haltingly over.

"I've never forced those people who've worked for me to have an injury attended. What I have done is explain why it's important that it's out," he added. "I could tell you about the horrible infection possible if you don't have it cleaned and cared for, but I'll spare you those details. Instead, as someone who's had entirely too many pieces of glass, brick, or wood slices stuck in my hands and other parts of my body, I can attest to how miserable it is when it's in, and yes, it's miserable getting it out, but then it's over, and you're free to use your hands." His lips quirked in a wry grin. "To throw snowballs without suffering as you do." Setting aside the case, Martin turned his palms up. "Either way, the choice is yours."

Her son hovered, uncertain and wary, and then, after several long beats of silence, he nodded and held his hand out to Martin.

With an infinite tenderness, Martin set to work examining her son, and as he saw to Logan's injury, he took care to tell him precisely what he was doing.

"I'm just going to begin by looking. I'm going to see where the glass is and how big the slivers are…"

Oh, goodness.

Her heart shifted in a way it hadn't in so long, in a way she'd not thought it could ever shift again, because her heart had been broken. But now, that organ galloped in her chest.

"The instant it is too much, you tell me, and I'll stop. We'll go slow."

Logan nodded once. "All right, sir."

Martin chuckled, and as he worked, he said, "I'm no sir. Never was. Just a common man. A builder from East London."

"My new uncle, Tynan, is from East London. Do you know him?" Logan asked as Martin picked up that metal device and ever so carefully proceeded to pluck out the tiny fragments that had become stuck in Logan's palm.

There was a simplicity to her son's wondering, one in which a child had no idea how big the world was and how unlikely it was two people from London would know each other, even if Faye's husband, a former warden at Newgate, had been well known among the criminal sorts. And yet, Martin proved kind and patient in that questioning. "Tynan?"

"Wylie," her son clarified, supplying the last name.

With the way Martin made a show of thinking on it, as though he truly searched his mind, it occurred to her once more how very wonderful he was with children.

More specifically, and even more bewitchingly for it, *her* children.

"No, I'm afraid I don't," Martin finally said.

He removed another shard, and Logan winced.

"But I do know someone with the name Tynan."

"Maybe it is the same?" Logan ventured.

"The Tynan I knew had a wooden leg."

Her son's interest piqued once more, and he widened his eyes. "Was he a pirate?"

"Nah. I told him he could tell everyone he was. We were friends as boys. His family lived next door to mine. We were close in age, but Tynan couldn't work because he'd been born without a right leg. Struggled to get around, he did," Martin said. "Limped everywhere. Fell down. Couldn't work... until I helped him out." Martin paused, just long enough to add a layer of intrigue.

"How did you help him?" Logan asked, and Martin dropped one of the pieces of glass on the edge of his nipper on the floor.

"I made him a leg."

The boy snorted.

"I'm serious," Martin said, stopping only long enough to lift his gaze and reveal the seriousness in his eyes.

Logan's eyebrows shot up. "Truly?"

"My da laid brick and worked for a builder, as did I. I always had a skill for designing and building, and one day, I had the idea to create a wooden leg for Tynan. I asked my employer, Mr. Webb, for leftover pieces to use to design several models."

Fully engrossed in that telling, Christina stared on with something akin to awe as Martin masterfully removed those pieces of glass from her son's hand, while Logan remained completely distracted.

At age seven, Martin had been overseeing those responsibilities better fit for a nursemaid or an adult?

"It took me several goes, and then… I did it. And now, Tynan works for me." Returning the nippers to his case, Martin removed a kerchief from his jacket and gently wrapped Logan's hand. "And there we are."

Logan widened his eyes and looked quickly from Martin to his injured palm and then back again at Martin. "I'm done?"

"We're done." Patting him gently on the shoulder, Martin nodded his chin toward the door. "I trust you want to run along and catch the rest of my brother's—"

Logan was already lifting his hand in a wave as he went racing off in the direction his siblings and Martin's brother had taken.

After he'd gone, leaving Christina and Martin alone, Martin straightened.

A weight of silence lingered in the air, periodically broken by the far-off murmuring of her children and Martin's brother in the distance.

She hovered, uncertain. It had been far easier when he'd been the surly stranger snarling at her children and not this.

Christina spoke at the same moment he did. "I cannot—"

"I'm sorry—"

He motioned for her to speak. "Please, you first."

"I was going to say thank you for tending his hand," she said softly. He'd shown her son a tenderness in caring for his injury that not even her late husband had. Certainly none of the men whom her family had invited as potential future husbands and fathers would have either. The reminder of why she was here at her mother's brought a wave of melancholy and regret.

Martin stepped closer. "What is it?" he murmured, lightly brushing his knuckles over her jaw, and her breath hitched.

The melancholy and regret came because she didn't want to be every woman requiring a fortune, willing to make an emotionless match. Nor did that sense of regret have anything to do with her late husband. Rather, it had to do with the fact that she remembered with Martin what it was like to have a shared connection with a man, and she'd not have that again.

His furrowed brow dipped. "Christina?" He spoke her name with a familiarity befitting two who'd known each other a lifetime and not only two days.

"Nothing," she said quietly, stepping away and dislodging his touch. "You were saying?"

A shadow fell over his eyes.

"I was apologizing for his hand getting injured. They are unfamiliar with this type of work, and I should have been more watchful because of that."

This was the only discussion that should exist between them, those details pertaining to the entire reason their paths had crossed and her reason for being here now. "No. They were responsible for this, and it was an important lesson learned."

He searched her face, and then that piercing stare fell upon her mouth, lingering there the same way it had when Lachlan had interrupted what had almost been a kiss between them.

Christina edged her chin up even as Martin lowered his slowly. Ever so slowly. His gaze remained on her lips, lifting ever so slightly to the bridge of her nose and then back again.

Closing her eyes, she tipped her head back.

"Mama, Mama, Mr. Phippen the smaller one is a hero!" That jubilant cry brought the world—and Christina—screeching back into the present.

Christina and Martin both jumped away from each other.

Whirling to face their audience, Christina prayed they'd failed to notice just how close they'd stood, and worse, how close she'd been to surrendering to this man's kiss.

"Is he?" Christina brought herself to ask, her voice slightly high and squeaky to her own ears.

Sprinting over, Luna hurtled herself into Christina's arms, and she staggered back slightly before planting her feet and folding her daughter's small form in an embrace.

"Oh, yes!" Luna exclaimed, yanking Christina's skirts as she spoke, each little tug a punctuation mark to her excitement. "He's been to *very* many places and fought old

Honey."

Befuddled, Christina gave her head a shake. "Honey?"

Luna nodded. "Honey!"

"Boney," Logan corrected with all the beleaguered tones only an older brother was capable of. "His name was Boney."

"Yes, yes. Him!"

"You don't even know who Boney is," Lachlan snapped as he and Logan and Mr. Thad Phippen joined them. "Doesn't seem you should be that excited about it."

Luna stuck her tongue out. "Yes, I can be. And I am." She returned her attention to Christina. "I like Mr. Phippen and the shorter Mr. Phippen."

"I do believe that's how I'm going to refer to my brother now. The *shorter* Mr. Phippen," Martin drawled, and both brothers made feinting motions as if sparring, and she found a smile twitching on her lips at that unrestrained closeness.

A laugh slipped out at the antics of the two gentlemen.

The hilarity of it was not lost on her either. Thad was just two inches shorter than Martin's impressive six feet, four inches. None would ever call either of the big, burly builders *short* or *small*. Yes, she well understood just how easy it was to like Martin Phippen and his jovial brother.

"Why are you staring like that?" Lachlan snapped, and Christina's face went hot, and her amusement ended abruptly.

"Probably because it's not every day she sees two grown men fighting," Martin supplied for her, and he ruffled the top of Lachlan's head with a familiarity and warmth that brought about those same odd sensations in her chest.

Her son scowled and ducked away from that touch.

"Don't mind him," Luna said. "He's just been angry since Papa died."

"Quiet your mouth," Lachlan shouted. "I'm not angry."

A pall immediately fell over the room, her daughter's comment a reminder that grounded each person present in reality.

Christina cleared her throat. "We should be returning," she murmured. And it was true. As it was, Christina's mother would be pacing at a window, awaiting her return so that Christina could get on with finding a husband.

Martin looked to her children. "You did good work here today," he said, and she couldn't help but feel forgotten. It was a reminder that his interest in her resided solely in the mess her children had made and that there wasn't really a connection with her.

"We shouldn't have had to work," Lachlan exploded. "It's your fault my brother got hurt, and it's not right for a little girl to be put to work."

Christina gasped. "Lachlan!"

Her son turned his ire on her. "And you shouldn't be friendly with a man who'd put your kids to work." With that, he stomped off.

Shame and mortification filled her. He'd become atrocious, and he was becoming worse in his fits and with his rudeness.

"Mrs. Thacker…" Martin began quietly, but she quickly cut him off.

"As I said, we should be going. My apologies for Lachlan's behavior," she said, avoiding Martin's eyes.

"Goodbye, Mr. Phippen," she said, and as she caught

Logan's and Luna's hands and allowed Martin and his brother to escort her and her three children out, she found herself with the feeling of loss that came in leaving, but also a sense of relief that Martin would not bear further witness to the mess that her life had become.

Chapter 7

Later that day, with the newly hired villagers arrived and put to various tasks throughout the stone manor, Martin stood at the long mahogany dining table, which he'd converted into a worktable.

With the pages spread out before him, Martin bent over those sheets, making design notes with changes—all the many changes—required of this place.

It was the kind of work Martin loved.

But he was also practical in the investments he took on. Unlike the wealthy merchant class, or members of the *ton*, Martin hadn't been born to wealth. Hell, he hadn't even been born to poverty. He'd been well below that. Every pence he possessed was a pence he'd earned. It's how he'd managed to rise up, and though he was not as wealthy as the powerful people he worked for, he was comfortable enough and on a path to even greater riches than he'd ever had—or more than any boy born to East London could hope to know.

That was why all he'd been able to see of his brother's purchase the moment he'd arrived was how much coin would have to be sunk into rehabilitating his new investment.

Until Christina had spoken.

I don't know what you are seeing, Martin... There are traces of the new world blended with that of the old. A perfect mix of what was once here and what could be again.

After she'd gone, he'd been enlivened in ways he hadn't been in so long because of a project.

More... because of her.

Nor did his distracted thoughts have anything to do with the decrepit state of the land and manor his brother had saddled them with.

Rather, it had to do with the woman who'd spent part of the morning here. A woman who'd spoken with the same manner of zeal and passion he knew for design. And a woman whom he'd almost kissed twice. And who, by the desire that had flickered in her eyes, had wanted that embrace as much as Martin had.

Unless he'd merely seen that which he'd wanted to.

Because—

"Well?"

His head came whipping up so quickly the muscles of his neck, tense from being bent in the same position for so long, screamed in protest.

Standing adjacent to Martin and his notes, Thad grinned. "I never thought I'd see the day when my big brother was woolgathering."

No, neither had Martin. "I'm working," he mumbled, which was as much true as anything.

"Are we finally going to speak on what that was?"

Baffled, Martin glanced down at the most recent annotations he'd made to the sheet in front of him.

Thad laughed. "I'm talking about your visit this morning, Brother." And in a display that showed he was entirely too comfortable and that he had no intentions of leaving, Thad dropped his hip on the edge of the table, folded his arms, and stared expectantly at Martin.

Oh, bloody hell. "My visit?" he hedged, searching for more time.

"You know," Thad said dryly. "The young mother."

Of course, his brother would not let this go. Tossing down his pencil, Martin tugged at his shirt collar. "The lady insisted her children clean," he said as casually as he could. "I told them not to touch the glass. And you saw, the boy was handling—"

"Not that," his brother said, his tone amused. "The other scene I came upon. You and Mrs. Thacker."

Oh, shite.

There was a beat of silence. "No."

"Fine." His brother paused. "Do I *need* to know?"

"You don't need to know anything about…" His relationship with the young widow wasn't… anything. In fact, this morning spent with her had marked the last he'd ever see her. "They aren't coming back. I think they learned their—"

Fishing something from the front of his jacket, Thad tossed it across the table.

The thick ivory velum landed with a loud *thwack*.

Furrowing his brow, Martin fetched the envelope and, sliding his finger under the black wax seal, unfolded the page.

"It's an invitation," he said, glancing up.

"From our neighbors. Our only neighbors here."

From Christina's family.

"They've welcomed us for the holiday party they are throwing."

"They've welcomed us." Martin barked his laughter, and he tossed the invitation back.

"Well, that's rude," his brother said with a frown.

"They're nobles. We don't mingle with nobles."

"You work for nobles. We work for the peerage," his brother amended.

Martin pounced on that. "Yes, that's correct. We *work* for them. We don't sip their brandy and dance at their balls. We meet with them during business hours."

Hopping up, Thad tossed his arms wide. "This is the country, Brother."

The country or Town, when it came to whom a rough builder from East London mingled with, it remained the same.

"I have it on the authority of the villagers whose services we've employed that the lady and her sisters are, in fact, ladies. However, her one sister's husband is an American. A painter. And the lady's other sister is married to a former prison warden at Newgate."

That gave him pause.

Both of those matches were unexpected for ladies of the peerage. And yet…

"We're not going," he said, and with a finality meant to end a discussion that wasn't really a discussion, he picked up his pencil and returned his attention to the parlor.

"Does this have anything to do with Mrs. Thacker?"

Heat splotched his cheeks.

"Because it doesn't matter if you don't like her. She is the sister of our family's neighbors, and given that you've put that lady's children to work for you, well, I should consider us fortunate for having secured this courtesy."

He stilled. Wait a moment. That was what his brother believed? That Martin didn't *like* Christina Thacker? A dizzying relief almost made him laugh.

"Martin?"

"Leave it be, little brother," he warned. "As it is, we've got a lot to do here. And we don't have the luxury of simply quitting our work and going to take part in a damned party."

"Do you have the luxury of angering potential clients?"

For a second time, he hesitated, his brother's question bringing him up short. Did he? Years ago, the answer would have been an absolute no. As it was, Martin had certainly built up a long enough resume of pleased clients, powerful people both of working-class origins who'd managed to make more for themselves and high-powered lords and ladies. But even with that, one who earned his own coin by the work he did for patrons had to always be careful. Luck could change. One or two bad words could have lasting consequences.

His brother smiled smugly. "I thought so," Thad said, and scooping up the invite, he tossed it over again, this time catching Martin in the chest.

Martin's hands curled reflexively around the thick paper.

"Either way, your feelings for the family aside, this house needs to be stocked, as you've pointed out. And the roof and windows fixed. We aren't going to have sufficient heat for at least several days. It makes sense to attend their house party if for no other reasons than those."

He hated that his damned brother was right on that score. Still, he dug his heels in. "We've dealt with cold before, Thad."

"I've already gone and sent 'round our acceptances." Pointing Martin's way, Thad waggled a finger in a small circle at him. "So, find your best dress clothes, big brother. We are joining the Grays for the holidays."

Not just joining the Grays. Rather, Martin would be joining the distracting and entrancing widow, Christina Thacker.

As his brother quit the room, Martin cursed.

The last thing he needed or could afford were any distractions she or her precocious, but equally endearing, children provided.

Chapter 8

She was in the wrong.

She'd been wrong in so many ways that morning where Mr. Phippen was concerned.

Her children had made a mess of his household, breaking his windows, destroying parts of his home.

He could have responded far worse than he had.

And she would have preferred it. She had preferred when he was the bellicose, surly stranger scaring her children, compared to the concerned gentleman who'd fished her out of the snow and dusted the remnants of those flakes from her cheek.

Because it was easier to be hated than pitied. And there could be no doubting that pity had precisely been the sentiment that she'd spied in his dark brown eyes.

It was the same blasted sentiment she'd seen in the eyes of so many people. Her neighbors in the village she used to call home. Her former servants. Her current nursemaid. Her siblings. Her siblings' spouses.

And now Mr. Martin Phippen.

Mr. Martin Phippen, who for a moment hadn't treated her as some poor relation or a sad woman to feel badly for, but rather, he'd treated her with real, honest emotion.

Nay, it hadn't been just pity. In a short time, they'd bonded, which made being near him impossible.

And which made her sister's announcement even more so.

"You did what?" she blurted.

Claire, fully engrossed in the Christmas scene she painted upon the canvas hanging in the hall, didn't so much as look up, lost in her project for the festivities as she was. In fact, Christina wagered her sister hadn't even heard her.

"Claire?" she prodded impatiently.

"A music performance with guests singing carols is perfectly appropriate," her sister said, and Christina stared at her incredulously.

"I am not taking exception to the music performance," she gritted out. Well, in some small way, she was. There'd be the expectation from Christina's mother that she'd perform, and as a guest in attendance at her sister's house party, she would have to.

There would be time enough for that misery after.

Claire paused and looked around.

Immediately, a servant came rushing over with a fresh palette of paints of different shades, which she exchanged with the young woman. With a word of thanks, Claire returned to the mural. For a moment, Christina thought her younger sister intended to ignore her question. Or mayhap, attending her project as she was, she'd simply failed to hear Christina's query.

"I'm afraid I'm not following. You're not complaining about the musicale, which means you're complaining about…" Her sister paused in mid-stroke of the holly bush she brought to life upon the canvas. "My guest list?"

"Yes. No. Not your guest list," she clarified. "Just…" Christina's lips pulled in a grimace. "One *person* on that list."

Her sister finally stopped attending to her project. "I'd not expect you, of all people, to have a problem with my including a neighbor who is of the working class."

"It's not that," she gritted out. It wasn't that, at all. She'd been the last one who'd ever cared about titles and money, as had been evidenced by her marriage to a struggling member of the gentry, who, once he'd fallen ill, had left Christina and their children destitute.

Her sister folded her arms and fixed a long stare on Christina. "Oh, then, what is it?"

"It's… it's…" she floundered.

Her husband's passing required that Christina marry for money and security, and she didn't want Martin Phippen, a respectable master builder who'd welcomed her views and been patient with her children, to witness her being a fortune hunter.

"Just… because we do not know him," she said weakly. The truth was, she didn't respect herself and the decisions she found herself on the cusp of making, and for reasons she didn't understand, it mattered to her that he not see that side of her.

"He is my new neighbor. At some point, we will know one another," Claire pointed out.

"I don't expect he even intends to stay. The property is merely a project."

Her sister swung her gaze back Christina's way. "And how do you know that?"

Christina froze, and she let loose a thousand black curses inside her head. "I... you said he was a builder," she finished lamely.

"And because he's a builder and a self-made man, you expect his only use for the property is as an investment that he'll sell, rather than making it his own residence?" Claire shot back. She didn't let Christina respond. "I am disappointed in you. I'd have expected such narrowmindedness from Mother, but not you."

It was on the tip of her tongue to explain that hers wasn't an opinion, but rather, a fact from her dealings with the gentleman. But that would also require her to share that which she was already desperately seeking to keep from her sister. From all of her family.

"Isn't it enough that I'm asking you not to invite him?"

"Well, I'm sorry to disappoint you, but I've already gone around and had an invitation sent."

"You've already invited him?" she bemoaned needlessly.

"I have," Claire said, affirming that truth anyway, speaking over Christina's groan. "The gentleman is perfectly lovely and polite, as is his brother. Not even Mother could take offense with their manners."

Oh, their mother *would* take offense to a man like Martin Phippen. Broad and strong, when gentlemen of the *ton* were either stuffed with padding or painfully thin. Direct and blunt, when most men didn't say what they were thinking to a woman. And then there was the simple fact, the only thing that truly mattered to a woman *like her mother*, that he wasn't of the *ton*.

She made another appeal. "He won't be comfortable

here, Claire."

Her sister gasped.

"I'm not being rude." She was being factual. "The guests here are…" Prim and proper and deucedly boring for it.

Claire winged an eyebrow. "Go on."

"They are… They are…" Here, knowing that Christina was looking for a husband among them. "They are of *elevated* rank."

Her sister's eyes bulged, and emitting a strangled sound, Claire shook her head.

"Yes, they are. And Mr. Phippen is not," Christina said flatly, settling into her argument, finding her legs as her sister now floundered. "He does not belong here." And in truth, he didn't. Not with the purpose of the party being what it was.

The palette slipped from Clair's fingers, splattering paint about the floor, and she instantly slapped her hands to her reddened cheeks. "Mr. *Phippennnn*…" Her sister's last syllable ended on a high-pitched squeak as she went flush in the face.

"Yes, I'm speaking of Mr. Phippen," she said impatiently, bending down to scoop up her sister's art supplies. "And I can say with absolute confidence he does not wish to be here. The guests here are…" Stodgy. "Lofty, and he—"

"No," Claire interrupted. "Mr. *Phippen*."

Kneeling on the floor at her sister's feet, Christina froze, and her stomach dropped.

Oh, God.

No.

Please, no.

It was a small appeal. The smallest of those she'd made over the years.

Alas, in all the previous instances, the Lord had provided unobliging, and as such, she should have expected he'd not intervene on her behalf this day.

Still, she clung on tight to hope for another moment. "Is he here?" she silently mouthed to Claire, praying. Still praying.

"He is," her sister returned in a soundless reply.

Oh, bloody hell.

Claire smiled, a more tense, strained one than Christina had ever before seen her sister don, and swept around Christina. "Mr. Phippen," her sister greeted jovially.

"A pleasure to see you again, Mrs. Gray."

That booming voice thrummed through Christina and held her motionless for altogether different reasons than the mortification that had paralyzed her.

As pleasantries were exchanged, Christina remained on the floor and made a show of fetching her sister's forgotten brush and resting it upon the clever little notch Tynan had carved into the palette, a gift he'd handmade for his sister-in-law.

Suddenly, two feet appeared before her, sliding into her line of vision.

She stared at those boots.

Those large—very large—boots.

The leather gleamed in ways, given her finances, she'd forgotten leather could shine.

Whereas Christina wore tired leather and would until she married again.

Suddenly, the urge to cry proved far stronger than her earlier embarrassment.

Martin stretched out a hand. "May I give you a hand, ma'am?"

"I do not need your help." Frustration, at her situation, at having been caught talking about him, pulled those six words from her, adding a sharp, shrewish quality to her tone that brought another gasp from Claire. "I have it just fine." And then, as she attempted to straighten, she lost her balance.

In one fluid motion, as the palette slipped from her fingers and before it could take another tumble, Martin caught it by the edge with one hand, and with the other, he looped an arm around her waist and prevented her from falling face first onto the floor.

Instead, she went sprawling against his chest, and the collision with a wall of muscle sucked the breath from her lungs the same way it would have had she landed on the ground.

Oh, my.

Claire rushed over and rescued her paints. "Thank you so very much, Mr. Phippen, for rescuing my paint and my sister."

Rescuing her sister.

With a droll grin, he touched a finger to an imagined brim. "I'm happy to assist. Even we nongentlemanly types are capable of assisting a lady," he drawled.

Nongentlemanly types.

Embarrassed heat filled her face. "That isn't what I said," she mumbled.

He arched an eyebrow. "No, I think it was something about elevated ranks and lofty guests? Wasn't it something to that effect?"

So he'd heard everything.

Splendid.

"Hmm?" he prompted.

"Given you clearly heard, I didn't think you required a confirmation on my part, Mr. Phippen."

She registered her sister's silence and round-eyed gaze at the same time, and there were entirely too many questions there.

"Ahem."

Grateful for that interruption, she looked over at Claire's housekeeper.

"Mrs. Gray, Cook has questions regarding the evening's menu."

"Please let her know I'll be along shortly," Claire said, and after the young woman had rushed off, Claire turned back to Martin. "If you'll excuse me, Mr. Phippen. I have some details I must see to. However, there are still refreshments in the breakfast room. I'm sure my sister would be happy to escort you there."

Martin and Claire both looked at Christina, and with them staring at her in expectant silence, it took a moment to register what her sister had said and, more horrifyingly, what was expected of her.

"I trust you can escort him," Christina blurted, catching her sister by the arm.

Martin's eyes narrowed even as her sister gasped.

Oh, hell. Her cheeks were going to be in a perpetual

blush. Christina relinquished her desperate hold on Claire. "That is, as it is on your way." With a forced smile, she stared intently at her sister, trying to will her to see and hear that silent appeal.

Claire gave her a peculiar look. "No, it is not."

Christina kept the pained smile on her lips firmly in place. "Isn't it?" she asked through that compressed, hard line. "Because I am *certain* it is."

Claire shook her head. "It is not. Actually, it is the opposite direction." As if Christina didn't have a clue what *opposite direction* meant, her younger sister stretched one arm one way and her other arm in the other so she stood there like a lowercase t.

"Oh, I must have been mixed up, then," she made herself say as breezily as possible. All the while, that entirely too-amused grin on Martin's lips widened.

He was enjoying her misery.

Granted, he should, given what he'd likely heard and the opinion he'd no doubt reached.

Claire turned another smile on their guest. "Again, Mr. Phippen, I'm so happy that you and your brother will be able to join us. As is my sister."

When Christina remained there in silence, Claire gave her a none-to-discreet kick to the shin.

"Delighted. Absolutely thrilled. Happy," she stammered, blushing under the latest knowing glance Martin slid her way.

Angling her head, Claire mouthed, "Behave and be nice."

"I am," she returned in like silence.

With that, her sister rushed off, and Christina and Martin were left alone.

In silence.

In a long, awkward, thick, uncomfortable silence.

He wasn't going to make this easy for her, then. Not that she'd expected he would.

Needing to be free of him, she gestured. "This way, Mr. Phippen."

Chapter 9

Martin wondered how long it would be before the lady spoke to him again.

Some five or so minutes later, with her marching at a clip to rival Boney on his retreat out of Russia, it became clear she'd no intention of saying anything.

"Since you pointed out my limited understanding of people in Polite Society, tell me, is it customary for a lady to run at a full sprint away from someone she's escorting to a breakfast room?"

For several moments, Christina continued at her brisk clip, and he thought maybe the distance she'd put between them had prevented her from hearing his dry query, but then she abruptly stopped.

Dropping her hands on generous hips—he was annoyed with himself for noticing—she turned and glared.

She did not, however, say anything in return.

Unlike yesterday and earlier today, when she'd been full of tart replies and garrulous about her views on his newly purchased properties, she remained stonily silent, and it was as though she were a different person, and he might as well have imagined those previous meetings.

Except, he hadn't.

What he had also heard, however, were her feelings on him and his station and her wishes about his being here. More specifically, her wish that he'd not attend the house party.

He hated he should care so much that she'd proven like so many other ladies of the *ton* who thought him inferior.

Martin reached her side. "I don't think I've witnessed you move this quickly, except when you were running away from my properties yesterday," he said, determined to get a rise out of her.

And failing.

Side by side, they walked the remainder of the way to the breakfast room. Coming to a stop, she gestured to the open doorway. "Here we are, Mr. Phippen."

Mr. Phippen again, was he?

He flashed a half grin. "We'd agreed to use one another's first names."

A pretty pink blush brightened her cheeks. "Hush," she returned, glancing around at the two footmen stationed in the breakfast room.

"Don't want me here, do you?" Martin drawled. "And here I'd thought we'd gotten past our initial hiccoughs to form a friendship."

"We are not friends," she said automatically. "We barely know one another."

And yet, she'd shared her passion for designing interiors with him, when she'd not even revealed that longing to her sisters.

"But we'd gotten on fairly well, all things considered," he said, his large legs instantly erasing the distancing between them as he approached.

"We did," she gritted out.

"But you don't want me here? I'm offended, Christina."

"Shhh," she whispered, slapping a hand over his mouth and then instantly drawing back her fingers.

Horrified for having touched him? With the important guests she'd spoken of being under this roof, he'd wager his business on that.

She looked about.

"Can't have your family knowing you're keeping company with a simple builder."

"I don't mind that you are a builder," she said tersely. "And there's nothing simple about you or the work you do."

"Why, thank you," he drawled. "How very generous of you."

She lingered there, biting at her lower lip, looking as if she wished to say more.

And he waited. Wanting her to. Because he didn't want this to be how their exchange went. Even as it shouldn't matter. Even as he shouldn't care.

And then…

"Goodbye, Martin," she said softly before stepping past him and heading off in the same direction they'd come.

He stood there until she turned the corner, her faded sapphire skirts fluttering as if issuing a final exchange.

He should be fixated on the exchange he'd stumbled upon between her and her sister.

And yet, his mind remained locked on just one detail.

Goodbye, *Martin*.

Not *Mr. Phippen*.

Martin.

The woman was a damned conundrum.

He didn't know whether she was the type to defy societal rules of propriety and decorum, having sent her children off to clean up after themselves. Or the sort who didn't want to mingle with a fellow outside of her station.

Either way, she wasn't his to sort out. He was here for a handful of nights at most, and then he'd head back to his various projects, and she'd go wherever she went after her sister's house party was at an end.

Giving his head a shake, Martin entered the breakfast room. Despite the late afternoon hour, the sideboard remained stacked with an impressive array of food items. Sugared confectionaries to rival those treats on display in the windows of London's finest bakeshops. Bread. Various meats and savories.

Making himself a plate, he carried it over to the empty table and claimed a seat.

One of the servants hastened over to provide a drink.

"Coffee, please," he said, discomfited as the young man poured him a cup.

The thing of it was, Christina hadn't been incorrect. He didn't belong here, and he didn't like mingling with the nobility. Oh, given that he worked for them, he knew how to move around them. But he'd never liked it. He was content to design for them and keep his relationships along that professional vein. This? Being served and treated like some manner of fancy gent? It filled him with unease.

With a word of thanks, he accepted the drink.

He felt a presence at the door and, along with it, an eager

anticipation. She'd returned.

Martin looked back.

"Oh," he blurted.

The little girl hovering there had at some point been swapped out of the coarse garments she'd worn while cleaning his corridors.

The condition of these garments, however, were not much improved. Though they revealed hints of long-ago quality, they also showed the same age and wear as the pants and jacket she'd worn earlier.

"Hullo, Mr. Phippen," the girl murmured.

Belatedly, he jumped up.

She hung there at the door, her gaze pointed at her small boots.

"It's good to see a familiar face," he said, and her head immediately came flying up.

It was as if his welcoming words had snapped across her reservations. The young girl came racing over, and as she did, she gave an exuberant wave for the pair of servants.

Before either of those men could, Martin drew out the chair next to him, and Luna flung herself into the mahogany seat.

Reclaiming the one he'd previously abandoned, he picked up his coffee.

"I saw you and my mama," Luna said without preamble.

He stilled.

What had she seen exactly? And when had she seen it?

"Oh," he said as casually as he was able.

"You were upset with her."

"Not at all." He'd been annoyed. Disappointed.

Luna dropped an elbow onto the table and rested her chin on her hand. "I know upset grown-ups, Mr. Phippen."

He matched the little girl's positioning and leaned down. "You? I can't believe you've angered a grown-up a day in your life."

"My grandmother," she said.

"Ah." This was the second mention of that woman. Given his experience with the peerage through the years, he'd met any number of harridans.

Luna remained silent, staring morosely at his plate.

Wordlessly, Martin shoved the delicate porcelain dish over.

Luna helped herself to the queen's cake and, not bothering with a fork, took a generous bite of the pastry.

"My ma didn't mean to be mean," she said around a large mouthful of food. "She's just mad because she has to get married again."

At that revealing admission from the guileless child, Martin stilled. "Is that right?" he said carefully, eager to hear more.

At the end of the table, the footmen tensed, clearly disapproving of Martin seeking information about the young widow.

Fortunately, in her innocence, Luna revealed no such awareness. "Mm-hmm." Luna considered his plate for several long moments and then looked up.

Again, Martin pushed it farther under her nose.

Smiling widely, Christina's daughter dropped the queen's cake and swapped it for a rich puff pastry. Tiny crumbs immediately flaked off the delicate pastry. "That's what Lachlan said, anyway. She doesn't like having to marry because she loved Papa, but *Grandmother* says she has to, because there are no funds and no future for her troublesome children if she doesn't."

Considering the impressive rote delivery of those latter words, it was a pronouncement the girl had heard uttered and often.

Across the room, one of the footmen coughed loudly.

"God bless you, Paul," Luna called over to the flush-faced servant.

Martin fought the smile pulling at his lips.

"Thank you, Miss Luna," the young man returned in pained tones.

Not missing a beat, Luna returned to the matter of her mother. "Mama has to listen to Grandmother this time, Logan said, because she doesn't like that we have to get our clothes and shoes and toys from Uncle Tristan and Aunt Poppy and Aunt Claire and Uncle Caleb. They give us gifts." As she spoke, revealing a wealth of information about the young widow and her family, Luna gesticulated with her pastry, those wild movements of her little limbs sending crumbs flying and falling. "Mama said our garments are just fine, and we don't need them, but I told her we like them, and our aunts and uncles like giving us gifts, and I don't see why we shouldn't take them."

"I don't either," he said quietly. "Family helps family."

Luna smiled and then snatched at the corner of her puff pastry with her teeth. "Eff-actly," she said, the sizable bite she'd taken converting her response into a barely intelligible mumble.

After she swallowed, her face fell. "But Mama doesn't like it. And so she has to marry. And I think she doesn't want you to see her having to get gussied up like a cock and preen."

Her little brow furrowed at the same moment his larger one did.

Then it hit him. "Peacock?"

She smiled. "Yes! That's what Logan said. A peacock."

With that, the little girl ceased the free-running supply of information about Christina and turned all her focus on the plate of desserts before her.

As she sifted through the pile, sampling several bites from each treat before moving on to the next, Martin considered everything the more-than-helpful girl had revealed about her family, and more specifically, Christina.

The family was in financial straits, then.

Having lived the first two decades of his life in poverty among other Englishmen, women, and children who struggled and starved, he'd simply assumed those born to the *ton* remained untouched by such troubles.

Sipping his coffee, Martin studied the top of Luna's bent head.

And no, Christina's situation wasn't entirely the same. She had wealthy family members with whom to find support. But she resisted that. Even as Luna had shared that her aunts and uncles had and continued to gift them with items, Christina insisted that her children wear the garments they did.

Pride was a sentiment that he, and any person in East London, could relate to. Having known winters when work was light for his father and family, Martin knew what it was like to have to beg. He'd done it. He'd had to accept those scraps, but he'd despised every moment of it.

A light touch landed on his arm, and he looked up.

Luna's little fingers, flaked with crumbs, rested on his coat sleeve, leaving little remnants of the pilfered treats upon the material. "I'm glad we broke your windows," she said softly.

"I'm glad you broke them, too." And he was stunned to discover he was. In just a couple of days, he'd come to appreciate the three troublesome children and their mother.

Luna smiled big. "*Lachlan* said I shouldn't make friends with you."

His lips twitched. "Did he?"

"Mm-hmm." She popped her fingers in her mouth one at a time and licked the sticky crumbs off of each little digit. "Because we won't ever see you again anyway, and you yelled at us. But I understand why you yelled at us." She paused and looked up. "We used to play with Papa like that. We'd throw snowballs and try to hit him. And Lachlan is *alwaaays* angry now," she said, squeezing several extra syllables into that overemphasized word. "So at first, I thought if we threw snowballs at your windows, Lachlan would be happy because he likes to break things, but then we saw you, and I had the idea to hit you, because then you'd have a snowball fight with us. Like Father," she added quietly, and then she stopped her rambling and hung her head lower.

Martin took in that explanation and the downcast, sad-eyed little girl before him.

And… something in his chest shifted.

A weakening.

He didn't want to feel badly for this family. Or worse, a connection. For that matter, after the walls Christina had thrown up a short while ago and her misbehaving children's complete disregard of his properties, he certainly didn't want to like them any more than he already did. In fact, when they'd stomped away in their neat little line yesterday, he'd been certain he never could or would.

From the moment Christina had run on excitedly about her visions for his properties, everything had gotten all twisted and turned upside down.

And then, Luna, aptly named with her full-moon-sized eyes, had spouted off about her and her family.

For he knew what loss did to a family. Martin knew how the absence of one member forever altered the fabric of a family, leaving it slightly more tattered than it had been before.

"I know something about snowball fights," he confessed.

Luna's head came up. Her eyes brightened, and she pumped her legs excitedly. "You do?"

"There were some cold winters in London when I was a boy. One time, the Thames even froze, and me and my brothers and sister skated upon it."

"You have a sister, too!" She dropped her chin into her palm and released a dreamy sigh.

"Had," he quietly corrected, before he could call the admission back. Because he really didn't need to speak about Alice with anyone. Because he hadn't spoken of her in years. Until this morning with Christina.

The light dimmed in Luna's blue eyes. "Did she die,

too?" she whispered.

He hesitated and then nodded.

The girl wrinkled her nose. "I *hate* death. Everyone dies." A worried glimmer filled her expressive gaze.

"Yeah," he said quietly. "They do." He waited until she'd shifted her attention back toward him. "The best you can do is love the people you love as best as you can every day that you can and enjoy every moment, not waiting for the worst to happen."

She cocked her head at a contemplative little angle. That slight tip of her neck sent several curls falling across her brow like a midnight-black curtain that obscured her vision. "I like that," she said softly. "You know, since Papa, I'm always afraid. I'm afraid something will happen to Mama. Or Lachlan or Logan." He opened his mouth to speak, but her musings kept coming, rolling together with the speed by which she spoke. "And you're right. Someday it will. But I'm always focusing on that. Maybe I shouldn't be. Maybe I should just enjoy the time we have." That endless stream of words came to a stop, and her high, heavily freckled brow dipped. "I try not to think about it, but sometimes I can't help it. I'll just be playing, and then I'll think, 'What if Lachlan is gone?'" She paused. "And Lachlan is really cranky a lot of times, so I sometimes think mean thoughts about Lachlan. And then I feel guilty for *thinking* mean things."

He leaned in. "Our brothers are always going to vex us."

The girl pulled her knobby knees up and drew them close. "You know something of that, too?" she ventured.

"You met one of my brothers," he reminded her. "Thad was the one responsible for buying that ramshackle property.

And it's only normal to sometimes think mean things about the people who vex us."

She smiled widely, displaying two rows of crooked teeth. "Indeed?"

Martin inclined his head in solemn acknowledgment. "Oh, absolutely."

"Well, I do think I like Mr. Thad's taste in buildings." The girl's generous smile wavered and then slipped like a star fading in the sky. "We vexed you," she whispered, her eyes stricken. "When we broke your windows."

"Yes."

Her wide mouth trembled. "D-did you wish bad things for us?" Her eyes met Martin's, and he kept his features set in a grave mask.

"I did."

She widened her eyes.

"Only that I had as an impressive arm to return a snowball in kind."

She giggled.

Martin split a confectionary treat in two, handing half over to the girl. "Truce?"

Luna stared with her perpetual wide-eyed wonder at the pastry and then dove into her piece. "Truff," she said around a mouthful of sticky bun.

While she devoured her share, Martin alternated between eating his and sipping his coffee.

They settled into a comfortable quiet.

The quiet proved short-lived.

"You know, you shouldn't be mad at your brother," she informed him with the same degree of seriousness and disapproval befitting a lecturing parent or nursemaid.

He dropped an elbow onto the arm of his chair. "Did I say I was mad?"

"No. But *he* said he found the manor, and you don't seem to like it."

"I like it," he said defensively.

Luna gave him a look.

"Oh, fine," he allowed. "But you have to admit that it is in a sorry state."

Luna again popped her fingers into her mouth, one at a time, licking the glazed remnants from those little digits. "Oh, no. Your house is quite magnificent."

"I've heard that before," he said wistfully. From the girl's own mother.

Everything from her dark curls to her fascination with crumbling properties marked the two as mother and daughter.

"You heard it from Mr. Thaddeus," she said.

"Yes, annnnd..." He paused for effect, and as the little girl leaned closer, he did the same. "Your mother."

Clasping her hands to her chest like she was herself a proud mama, Luna smiled broadly. "I *knew* Mama would love it." She released another sigh, her gaze taking on a far-off quality. "It looks like the castle in a book she reads to me at night about Sir Lancelot and Guinevere." Luna let her arms fall and spoke in a conspiratorial whisper. "My aunt Claire *thinks* her home looks like a castle."

Martin did a sweep of the elegant breakfast room, fine enough and styled enough to meet any London townhouse. "And do you?" he asked.

The little girl dropped her voice another fraction and leaned in. "It's pretty, but it's not like a perfect castle, because her and Caleb already fixed it up. But your castle is still blank, and you can make it your own."

He stared at her for a moment, recognizing that glimmer and, more, recognizing that eager quality in her words, words not dissimilar to the ones he'd had as a boy when he'd dreamed of doing precisely what he now found himself doing in life. "Tell me, Luna, what would you do to the manor?" he asked, putting the same question to her that he had Christina.

She blinked those enormous blue eyes several times and then touched a hand to her heart. "You are asking... me?"

Martin's lips quirked at the corner. "And should I not?"

"Well, Lachlan and Logan would say you shouldn't." Her nose scrunched up in distaste. "Because I'm a little girl, and I don't know as much as I think I do." With the ease with which she spoke those words, they were ones she'd heard directed her way numerous times before. "Not Lara," she said. "She's my baby sister."

The other child Christina had spoken of. So many children for a young woman to raise alone. So many children for any parent to raise. Her need to marry made all the more sense.

"She's almost one," Luna said.

Another painful vise squeezed about his chest. The husband hadn't been gone long, then. What must it be for Christina to balance her grief with the responsibilities she had?

"Lara doesn't ever have anything bad to say," Luna piped

in. "Though she doesn't really say anything at all yet. She just babbles things that don't make sense."

He grinned. "Tell *me*, then?"

"I'd have big wooden furniture. Big wood tables." She stretched her arms wide, visibly straining under her attempt to illustrate the enormity of that size. "So long. Like the kind the knights would all meet around. And tapestries, but not like Aunt Claire's with flowers. But old-looking ones with knights fighting and courting ladies."

She spoke with such zeal he found his smile growing. Yes, there could be no doubting she'd been bitten by the same love and passion for interior design as her mother.

"Oh, you absolutely must have red carpets on the stone floors, but don't cover them all!"

"Red carpets?" It was an unexpected request from a little child.

"Yes, so that when you play sword battles on them, you can collapse and pretend it's blood." With that, Luna sprawled back in her seat and flung her right arm wide while her left hand came up to clutch at her heart "Uuuugh," she groaned.

Martin inclined his head with the solemnity Luna's ideas merited. "Those are some very good suggestions," he murmured, rubbing at his chin. "I will be sure to take your design ideas into serious consideration and adapt them to my current plans."

The little girl instantly sprang upright. "Truly? You must let me see when you are finished." Her face fell. "Except, I'll be gone," she whispered. "And we'll never see you again."

Something shifted in his chest. "Well, it isn't forever,

right? I am your aunt and uncle's neighbor for now, and you'll surely visit again, and as long as I own the property, your family is welcome to visit. And when I have those red carpets installed, I'm going to make sure you have that sword fight."

Until he sold the property. And then some other nobleman would own the place, and that would be the end of Martin's time here and the end of his interactions with Christina and her children.

Luna tugged at his sleeve, drawing him back from those melancholy musings. "Truly, Mr. Phippen?"

It was unlikely they'd meet again, and the truth of that only added to the tightening in his chest.

"Truly," he promised, mustering a smile for her benefit. "And you can call me Martin. All my friends do."

Luna's smile returned, and then her gaze landed on something past his shoulder. "Mama!" she exclaimed.

His heart thundering under that pronouncement, Martin followed Luna's stare over to the doorway.

His gaze collided with the silent figure standing there.

Martin promptly stood. "Mrs. Thacker," he greeted.

***

She'd not intended to return to the breakfast room.

Not after their volatile exchange.

Nay, she'd stalked off, determined to spend the next week of her sister's house party avoiding him.

There was certainly enough space.

And certainly more than enough guests with whom to

occupy her time, all potential future husbands who were certainly less surly, and less angry, and less blunt.

But ultimately, she'd had to find her way back to the same room she'd stormed out of.

Because she'd not been able to let him believe she'd meant to be snobbish.

It would have been easier to just let the exchange between them end as it had, with him taunting and her aloof. After all, what did it matter if he thought she was one of those pompous ladies? They were basically strangers and wouldn't see each other again beyond this house party. And yet, as she'd headed off to do the task her sister had assigned her—making festive wintertime floral arrangements—she'd found it did matter. It mattered very much.

And then she'd found him with Luna, so engrossed in a discussion with her daughter—one that she'd refused to let herself interrupt—that she'd simply stared on, watching the two of them together.

He'd allowed Luna the dream of a future of building and designing, just as he'd done with Christina. He'd encouraged her to freely speak of her dreams and hadn't sought to squelch those dreams, instead indulging them.

Her daughter jumped up from her seat and raced over, flinging herself into Christina's arms. "Mama, I've had the most fun with Martin."

"Have you?" she murmured, holding her daughter against her and stroking her back.

Martin bowed his head. "We both did."

Two dimples appeared with Luna's wide smile. Her daughter puffed out her chest with pride. "I've given him design ideas, and he said they are very good, *aaand* he is going to use them."

Christina proved unable to keep her gaze from sliding over to the man who'd so captivated her daughter. "Did he?"

"She's got a great vision in terms of maintaining the historical integrity of a structure."

Angling back, Luna looked up at Christina and flashed another uneven smile. "Did you hear that? I have vision for storical integrate?" Her little brow furrowed, and she looked back at Martin. "What is that?"

"It means you don't try to make an old house new. You respect the stories that lived in them and try to keep true to how they used to be." Martin supplied that answer so perfectly, as though it was the most natural thing in the world to clarify difficult details for little children.

That was what Christina had wanted so desperately, for her children to have that kind of relationship with their father. Briefly, they'd had such a bond, but it had been so short, with most of their memories filled with him being sick. And now, there'd never be that again. Soon, there'd be a different husband, a man who was still a stranger to Christina, who'd give her security and provide for them. That he'd see her four children as his own, bonding so with them, sounded as elusive a dream as sliding down a rainbow and landing in the pot of gold at the end of it.

"Don't you think that is great?" Luna's question slashed across those heartbreaking musings. Before Christina could answer, her daughter tugged at her hand, bringing Christina's attention down. "Martin thinks I have great ideas."

"Of course I do, poppet. I think it is the best," she said,

her voice thick with emotion.

Luna's brow grew more quizzical. "Then why do you look like that? Like you just found out Da died?"

That question kicked Christina squarely in the chest. Nay, not just the question, the truth behind just why Christina felt that pressure and pain. Because, oddly, the realization of what she was about to do—marry again, for security this time—and what she'd never have, felt like a death of a different sorts.

"Not sad," she said, tugging one of Luna's curls, lying. Eager to shift them out of this sad talk, she said, "Your cousins are looking for you." Luna was usually eager to join Tristan and Poppy's daughters, so Christina could always count on that as a distraction for her, and one that would bring her happiness that Christina found herself increasingly incapable of providing her children.

"They are?" Luna asked excitedly.

"They are."

Except, instead of rushing off, Luna turned and ran back to Martin's side. "But that means I have to leave Martin."

Christina took in the man beside her daughter. The sight of his strength and the beauty of his masculine physique sapped the moisture from her mouth. No man had a right to look as he did—strong and powerful and like those bronzed statues lords and ladies spent good coin on to collect for their homes.

Christina forced her attention back to Luna. "I trust Mr. Phippen would welcome a spot of quiet." She held her arm up, but a recalcitrant Luna frowned and gripped the arm of her vacated seat in a clear hint that she had no intention of quitting it.

"Oh, no. Mr. Phippen likes my company, isn't that true?" Luna turned that question on the gentleman.

"Absolutely."

"He invited us to visit when we come back, Mama."

A swell of emotion formed a ball in her throat. Christina curled her fingers and toes sharply. "Did he?" she asked, her voice slightly pitchy as she slid her gaze to Martin once more.

Their gazes locked. "She's a natural inclination and ability when it comes to design ideas."

"D-does she?" Christina murmured, her eyes moving back to her beaming daughter.

"Absolutely," Martin said. "And it would be a shame if she didn't assess my final work, to be sure it fits with the vision she laid out."

"*Seeee*, Mama?"

"I do," she managed to get out through a still-thick throat. And she did see. She saw that her children deserved to have someone who respected them as people and made them feel wanted.

While an excited Luna proceeded to chatter away, sharing all the wonderful praise Martin Phippen had heaped upon her, the most glorious, lighthearted warmth filled Christina's person. A sensation she'd never thought to again know. Even as loving and devoted a father as her late husband had been to their children, he had not entertained the same dreams for their daughter that Luna had expressed. He'd cherished her, treating her like a princess who would one day be looked after, while the idea of her aspiring to anything beyond that status hadn't even been considered.

"I get my design ideas from Mama," Luna was saying, and Christina came jolting back to the moment. "My mama is very skilled at drawing houses and designs within them." Laying a hand on Martin's, Luna repeated in solemn tones. "Very skilled."

A wave of heat flooded Christina's cheeks. "Luna," Christina said on a rush.

"I believe it." Martin looked upon Christina with interest, and Christina's blush fired several degrees warmer.

"I'm really n—"

"Oh, yes. Very much so." Christina's garrulous daughter, absent of any kind of filter, proceeded to praise Christina's skills to one of London's most extraordinary and successful builders. "My aunt Claire draws people, but Mama can draw annnnny house or building. We draw together and pretend we have money to make our houses exactly as we want them."

Mortification stabbed at her breast. "That is enough, Luna," she said sharply, and all the excitement died in her daughter's eyes, the happiness brimming within a sentiment that had been missing so much since her father's passing. Nay, long before that.

"Luna," Christina said softly. It was too late.

Her daughter's lower lip trembled, and then she sprinted around the chair Martin had been sitting in, accidentally knocking into it, sending the seat into a noisy tumble.

Christina stretched a hand out to halt Luna's retreat, but the little girl evaded that touch and flew past.

The pair of servants in the corner, Paul and Willis, exchanged a look. The two footmen had been like playmates to her children since they'd arrived.

Willis cleared his throat. "Should we—?"

"If you would?" she asked, and with a quick bow, the two men immediately rushed off, setting off in pursuit of Luna.

With the room emptied of all but one other, Christina stood there, her back to Martin as she clenched and unclenched her hands into tight little fists. With her feet frozen to the floor, she could not make her legs move.

Because she found herself bungling everything so much, in ways she never had before.

Before, she'd been more patient. More lighthearted. More everything that had been good.

Everything that had already been hard had become exponentially so since her husband's death.

For an all-too-brief time, she'd had a partner, and she'd not properly appreciated just how much she'd needed that support until it had been gone.

"It's all right. We all have our moments." Martin spoke in the same soothing tones she used with her children when they were upset, and she bit her lower lip.

We all have our moments. She found herself having too many of them. With her children. With him.

"It's not, though," she said, more sharply than she'd intended, and then she immediately regretted that impatience. She closed her eyes. "Forgive me."

"Nothing to forgive, Christina," he said gently. "I've been known to bellow like a bear and deliberately scare children." He spoke without inflection. "You certainly didn't do that."

At the almost-teasing echo of words she'd hurled in anger at him not even a day ago, Christina ran a weary hand down the side of her face.

The fight went out of her, and the pride she'd clung so desperately to went right out the window behind it.

She let her shaking hand fall to her side. "I do that too often," she confessed. "I snap." To give her fingers something to do, to give herself a task so that she could be matter-of-fact, Christina righted the chair Luna had knocked over in her flight from the room. A nervous laugh spilled past her lips. "You saw that."

"You mean when you were escorting me here earlier?"

She winced. "Yes, that." She drew in a deep breath and said that which she'd come to say. "I am sorry you heard my exchange with my sister."

He stiffened, and she grimaced.

"That is, I'm sorry because I didn't mean those words the way they sounded, and I know how they *did* sound," she said, unable to stymie her rambling. "Because that is how my mother sounds, and I don't feel that way. About you. That is, that you are inferior," she hurried to clarify. "I don't believe that. At all." He'd proven himself in just two days to be far greater than all the gentlemen she'd met in her Come Out. Those stuffy prigs had made it altogether too easy to ignore her mother's plans for her marital state and to forge a future with a man of modest means. "I think—"

Suddenly, he touched two fingers to her lips, stopping her from rambling.

"It's fine."

Only, it wasn't.

"Why are you being so nice to me?" she whispered. After her children had wrought havoc on his household, and he'd stumbled upon her seemingly rude feelings to his presence. No doubt, he was being nice because of that emotion called pity, which she so deserved.

He ran those same two, long fingers over her cheek. The pads, callused as they were, lent his touch an intriguing blend of coarseness and tenderness, and it stirred feelings she ought not feel again. "Luna put me in my place. Reminded me my hurt pride blinded me to why you were saying the things you were."

Why she'd been saying the things she had…

Luna had told him…? Oh, God, what had Luna told him?

Martin continued to trace her face with his gentle touch. "She mentioned you are husband hunting here."

Oh, God.

Not for the first time that day, or even the second or third time with this man, Christina yearned for the earth to split itself wide and pull her down to escape… this.

"She said too much," she muttered.

"Did she speak the truth?" he asked.

Yes.

But how to admit that to this man?

Only, why was he any different? Every other guest knew the whole purpose of this party. His knowing, however, seemed somehow different.

Unable to bring herself to lie to him, Christina offered a tight nod and braced, waiting for him to judge her.

Chapter 10

A woman so proud as to prefer that her children and herself continue to wear aging garments instead of gifted newer ones would only ever struggle with such an admission, and yet, she'd made it anyway.

It spoke once again to Christina Thacker's character.

She clasped her hands before her. "You aren't judging me."

Hers wasn't a question. Rather, it was a statement packed in perplexity.

"Why would I judge you?" he replied.

"Because I expect you might feel a certain way about"—the lady's lips pulled like she'd taken a bite of the lone lemon tart remaining on the array of treats on the sideboard—"a fortune hunter."

Aye, on the surface, a woman marrying a man for no reason except for his money sounded callous and cold and unfeeling. Except, he'd had enough experience in his thirty-five years to know nothing was black-and-white. There was a spectrum of grays greater than most even knew existed beyond one single color.

"I've been hungry, Christina. I've been cold. I've been tired from having to work endless hours in the coldest winters and under the hottest suns only to find myself with a half pence for those efforts. I'd never judge anyone for what they do in the name of surviving."

She glanced down at her clasped fingers, studying those digits like they contained the answer to life before hesitantly bringing her gaze back to his. "Hearing you say that, speaking of what you've known, I trust it makes my view of financial struggles all the worse."

"My experience doesn't diminish yours." He dropped a hip on the table. "And also, I was able to find my way. To build my business and earn my fortune. I know enough of the world to know it doesn't permit women those same opportunities. And in that, she is a prisoner in ways that even a man born outside the peerage never is and never will be."

Christina's jaw slipped, and her lips moved, but no words came out. "I have never in my life heard a man speak so," she murmured. "My brother is devoted and supports his wife's passions and desire to pursue art, but even so, I've never myself heard him…" She paused as if searching her mind. "Or anyone, for that matter, say what you have."

He shrugged. "I'm just speaking the truth. I have men, women, and children in my employ. I'm well aware of what each of their circumstances are and can recognize the unfair disparity between men and women."

"Thank you, Martin, for being more forgiving than I deserve."

He brushed off that gratitude, and as that apology put an end to the discussion that had kept her here this long, Christina glanced over her shoulder toward the doorway.

He braced for her to leave. Wanting her to remain, because even as a man like him couldn't be more different than a lady such as her, there was an ease in being with her.

She looked back his way. "I have been charged with creating floral arrangements for the festivities."

At her low whisper, he leaned in, touching a finger to his ear, thinking he'd misheard that abrupt and unexpected shift.

She raised her voice a fraction, but still spoke in a hushed way. "My sister has asked that I see to the greenery that will be hung throughout her household. She says it is because of my skill with it. However, I think it is in large part because she's keeping me away from our mother."

"She's that bad?" he asked, his lips quirking in a smile.

"Worse," she muttered.

They shared a grin.

Hers slipped into a more serious line that she dampened with the tip of her tongue. His gaze locked on that tiny sliver of pink flesh, and he followed the path it trailed, his body stirring.

"Would you like to accompany me?" she asked, startling him from his wicked musings. He snapped his head up. "Forgive me," she said on a rush, misunderstanding the reason for his startlement. "I just thought that—"

"No," he said quickly. "I'd enjoy that."

She peered at him. "You *would*?"

He'd enjoy being with her. That detail he took care to omit and instead stuck with the safer truth. "I don't know a soul here, other than my brother, who's gone absent." Conspicuously so. "I'd welcome the opportunity to also hide."

Her smile widened, that generous glimmer of happiness climbing all the way to her blue eyes and wreaking havoc on a different part of his body—his chest.

"Splendid!" she said, giving her hands a little clap. And then, spinning on her heel, she bustled off, pausing only when she reached the doorway to look back to see whether he followed. "Well, now, have you changed your mind?"

He should.

Mingling with a lady who by her own admission was in the market for a wealthy nob of a husband at the very event Martin now attended seemed the height of folly.

Her brow slipped. "Martin?"

Alas, it was just a short while, and then that would be the extent of their time alone together at the house party, which would soon be filled with games and gatherings of large groups of people. "Coming," he said, and her smile was instantly restored.

They fell into step, with Christina leading the way.

As they walked, there was a companionable silence, and he took in the surroundings of her sister's household, a safer venture by far than thinking about Christina and the husband-hunting quest that would unfold.

The walls, done in the same stone as his, gave this household a similar old feel as the one Martin's brother had purchased on their behalf. The side chairs and sconces and side tables lining the halls were perfectly current pieces that added an air of modernity, melding an old world with a rapidly changing new one.

"What are your thoughts?" Christina asked, and he did not pretend to misunderstand her question.

"I think your daughter has an eye for design."

"Do you?" she asked, her eyes glimmering with pride.

He nodded. "She gets that from her mother."

A blush filled her cheeks. "You're being po—"

"Polite?" he interrupted with a snort. "Nah. I'm a builder, from a different station. I'm not inclined to go around handing out false compliments. Especially on matters of design," he added.

They reached the end of the hall, and he stopped. His gaze locked with hers. "She was correct in her assessment of what my properties should incorporate, and you revealed that same passion and vision."

Her hands immediately went to her heart. "No one has ever said I have vision," she whispered, passing her eyes over his face in the same way he now studied hers.

Like a moth to the fatal flame, his eyes went to her lips. She wet them once more. Her lashes fluttered, and he saw the same desire that was coursing through him reflected in the subtle nuances of her body's slight movements.

Martin lowered his head just as she raised hers—

"Christinnnaaaa!"

The lady gasped. "Bloody hell," she whispered, looking in the direction from which the shrewish query had come.

He lifted an eyebrow. "The worse?" As in, the mother.

A laugh burst from her lips, and she promptly slapped her palm over her mouth.

It proved too late, however.

"Christina, I hear you." That slightly whiny voice grew more strident, laced with frustration and disapproval.

"The worse," Christina whispered, confirming his supposition that the lady's mother was, in fact, the woman bearing down on her.

"Where is she?" Those mutterings came closer.

With an impressive curse, Christina took Martin by the hand and wordlessly tugged him along. She moved with the same agility of her precocious children when they'd been darting and dashing about his property yesterday, and he gathered now just where they got their impishness.

He allowed himself to be pulled along, happy to go, as it promised him freedom from the other posh guests with whom he'd eventually have to mingle.

Don't be a bald-faced liar to yourself, a silent voice needled at the back of his brain. *You know you're having a deuced good time with the lady.* This, when he'd not thought women of her sort knew a damned thing about fun. He'd taken them all largely to be like the mother they now evaded.

By the fading words her mother called out, they'd managed to elude her.

Slightly out of breath and laughing, Christina skidded to a stop, halting their forward flight beside an arched wooden door. Notches covered the curved panel.

"This is my favorite part of my sister's home," she said as she caught the wide rusted ring that bespoke the age of the artifact and gave a tug. "Because of the door," she went on to clarify, stepping inside the room.

Martin followed her in, and Christina reached back to draw the door shut, closing them in… alone. "Because of the door?" he asked, intrigued.

Christina headed over to a row of hooks beside the doorway, and as she fetched a simple white apron with a front pocket and donned the article, he could not take his eyes from her. "I believe it is original," she explained.

"It is," he confirmed. The age of the wood and the ornamentation all marked it as an item of long ago.

Christina beamed. "I thought as much." In the midst of attempting to tie the apron strings behind her, she paused, and her gaze grew far away. "It is as though the remnants of an older life were slowly taken over, stone by stone, hall by hall, and this doorway hung on, retaining a place here, too strong and bold to be removed and determined to remain like a beacon of another time amidst the newer."

She'd been bit by the architectural bug. And he'd never known a woman to wear that look before. Never before had he seen the eager excitement that now lit Christina's entire face, the spark within her eyes so bright, it was as though it had illuminated her from the inside out, a product of another person's property. He found himself bewitched all over again. Entranced.

Yes, he'd worked for and beside women who'd commissioned him to convert their properties, even a music hall in one case. But those had been places those clients had owned, not a general piece of architecture. Christina saw inherent beauty in something she had no emotional attachment to.

Suddenly, she drew her head back slightly and blinked slowly, and it was like the pull of her introspection had been shattered. Clearing her throat, she resumed the process of trying to tie her strings. "I trust you think it silly," she said, fiddling with those long laces. "Me speaking about doorways having personal attributes."

"I don't," he said with a solemnity born of the truthfulness of the words he spoke. "I think it makes sense. I understand it," he said. And he did. "My family lived in a one-room household," he confessed.

Christina ceased playing with her apron strings and turned to face him. "Did you?" she asked softly.

He managed a tight nod. "Aye." He continued on, moving her—and him—away from those uncomfortable parts of his past and on to the reason for his telling. "We had this one wall... My da would mark the heights of me and my three siblings with an old knife, and then beside each little line, he'd include our initials." She attended him eagerly, and he warmed to his telling. "He began when we were babes first able to stand, and then at each birthday, he'd mark our growth." He stared off at the wood table strewn with greenery and bows and beads and holly, his gaze locking on those items, though not really seeing them. "That wall bore the story of our growth and showed the time when my sister Alice's height ceased to be a mark with mine and my brothers. They eventually turned that house into a shop, and one day, I went in to find... that sole wall had managed to stand, and it bore the memories of mine and my siblings' past and story." He shifted his gaze back and found Christina staring at him raptly. He searched for a hint of pity at what he'd revealed but found none.

"That is what buildings and the pieces within them do, Christina," he murmured, resisting the urge to stroke her cheek once more. "I understand that more than anyone. Buildings are to be respected."

"That is beautiful," she whispered.

She'd seen beauty in that telling, and he was awed not

for the first time by the lady. For years, he'd taken care to keep those humbling details about his past from his clients. Lords and ladies didn't want to think the man they'd hired came from squalor or had had dirt as flooring. It would have sullied their opinions about the capability of his visions.

But she wasn't a client.

She was a woman here to make a match with some fine lord.

It was why he should go. It was why he should hurry up and end this exchange with her and seek out his rooms and hide there until he was forced to take part in whatever festive events his host and hostess had planned.

"Here." He came over, and when he reached boldly for the laces at her back, she tensed. Martin gave a light tug and made to fold one over the other. But then he stilled…

Close as he was, he was aware of the slight uptick in her breathing, of the rapid rise and fall of her chest. And his hands shook slightly as he forced himself to focus on the mundane task. He briefly closed his eyes. Only to be distracted by the smell of her—lemon and apple, scents so clean and also sweet upon her. Martin took a deep breath, filling his lungs with her scent as he managed to finish tying her strings in a neat bow.

"There," he murmured, releasing the laces. He should step away.

He expected she would.

Only, Christina remained there, and then she tipped her neck slightly.

And it was as though his body was perfectly in sync with her every move as he lowered his nose close to that long, graceful arch, breathing deep of her once more.

"What are we doing here?" He asked that question into the quiet previously punctured only by his and her breaths coming heavily in unison.

Angled as she was, he caught the downward sweep of dark lashes that went on forever and the way she dampened her mouth. He'd come to learn in a short time that she did that when she was nervous. Or when she yearned for a kiss.

Which was it in this instant?

Chapter 11

What were they doing here?

They were supposed to be designing festive arrangements for her sister's house party.

They were supposed to be hiding away from Christina's mother.

But it was all confused at the moment, in her mind, between what she was supposed to do and what she wanted to do. *In every way,* a voice taunted.

All her muscles stilled at that thought, and her mind balked, shying away from the reminder that even though she'd lost so very much, she wanted more. She wanted to live her life fully again. She wanted a happy life that saw her not with a man who provided a purse and nothing more, but with one who saw her as a life partner.

In ways not even her own husband had.

She wanted to be happy again.

And she wanted the kiss that had been hovering in the air between them since early this morning.

Even as it was dangerous.

Even as she knew her role and her responsibilities to her children.

She wanted this moment with him, Martin, for herself.

So, she might steal it away, tuck it in a private place only she knew of. When life was lonely and dark, she might pull it out and remember that there'd been a time again when she'd known passion and lived in a moment for herself.

Martin stroked a palm along her cheek, and she leaned into his touch, her body unwittingly offering him that signal of what she wished, letting him know, if he should so wish it, as she did, that in this instant she was as much his as he was hers.

His eyes darkened, his dark lashes descended, and then he claimed her mouth.

A soft sigh slipped out, and she melted against him.

He was there to catch her, looping a strong, powerful arm about her waist and drawing her against him. And she leaned against Martin, stealing also of the warmth and strength he offered.

As she climbed her hands about his neck, twining them about, clinging to him in a way that should have shamed her if she'd been capable of that useless sentiment in this moment, Christina pressed herself against his barrel chest and surrendered to his kiss.

He made love to her mouth with a tenderness that sucked the breath from her lungs, each glide of his mouth a gentle stamp upon her flesh that heated her from within. Those flames fanned out until the fire grew, and he deepened his kiss, the meeting of their lips stoking the rapidly spiraling inferno.

Martin's fingers tightened upon her hips, his fingers curling sharply through the fabric of her dress and into her skin, almost reflexively, and he immediately gentled his touch.

Only, she whimpered, craving the raw volatility of his touch, wanting him unconstrained and free with his caresses and his desire.

Then, as if following those silent, secret yearnings, he slid his hands around her and over the swells of her buttocks, drawing her ever closer until she felt his shaft, hard against her belly.

She moaned, the evidence of his desire fueling her own, and Christina moved rhythmically, shamefully… wantonly against him.

Only, no, there was no shame in her body again knowing passion.

She'd not allow that emotion to enter. Not this.

Martin drew one hand away, and she whimpered in protest at the loss of his touch. Except, he shifted that caress, guiding those same, long, callused fingers along her cheek, urging her with his tender touch to open for him.

And she did.

Christina let her lips part, and he slipped inside, his tongue sweeping against hers.

He groaned. That deep rumble shook his chest, the reverberations shaking her own, moving through her.

She angled her head to better receive him.

Suddenly, Martin wrenched away, and she sagged, silently crying out at the sudden loss of him as he ripped away from her that glorious taste of desire. Her body ached. Her fingers shook.

"What—?" she asked through the haze of passion, wholly incapable of forming a coherent thought.

He only moved farther away from her, putting several paces between them, and she wanted to weep for him to return to—

Creeeeeak.

The rusted hinges of the door groaned their way across her muddled thoughts, and Christina blinked.

"There you *arrre*."

If there was anything that could kill joy and desire and anything good, that was the voice to do it.

"I've been looking for—" Her mother abruptly stopped, her words and her steps, as her gaze landed on Martin.

The dowager baroness narrowed her eyes upon him, as she did with all those whom she deemed below her rank and worth—which was invariably most, and certainly this man, one of the working class.

Martin dropped a respectful bow that her mother completely ignored.

"I've been looking for you, Christina," her mother resumed in the cold, frosty tones that Christina believed were the only ones her last living parent was capable of.

She'd never liked her mother. She resented her for treating Christina's husband as an inferior because of his lack of title and wealth. And in this moment, Christina hated her with all she was worth for failing to so much as acknowledge Martin. Martin, who stood stoic and silent.

"And you've found me," she said, spreading her arms wide. "Claire asked me to create a floral arrangement, and *Mr. Phippen*"—she placed a sharp emphasis on his name as she motioned to him, forcing her mother to acknowledge his presence—"was good enough to offer his assistance."

Her mother's nostrils flared, making her already-sharp nose a touch pointier, giving her the look of the witch she was.

"My lady," Martin said with another bow, a second courtesy of which her mother was completely undeserving.

"Mr. Phippen," the baroness said, her greeting terse and coming as though dragged from her. Which in a way, it had been. Then she turned, cutting him with her shoulder and redirecting all her attention to Christina. "However, I took the liberty of having the children's governess gather them, and they will be coming shortly to assist you, along with several other… guests."

Guests. As in potential husbands.

Her insides spasmed.

"You needn't have done that," she bit out through her teeth.

"Oh, trust me, I very much needed to." The pointed look and edge to that pronouncement left no doubt as to the meaning.

Through it, Martin remained a silent observer to their exchange.

She'd loved everything that had come before this hideous moment, but she hated everything that had come after just as much.

"I should go," he said quietly.

"No!" she exclaimed.

"I think that would be a wise idea, Mr. Phippen," her mother said over Christina's almost-pleading rejection. "My daughter has other guests to entertain, and I trust you and your brother would feel more comfortable spending time with my sons-in-laws, Mr. Wylie and Mr. Gray." As in, those two sons-in-law born outside the peerage who'd had the audacity to marry her daughters and who, because of their work and backgrounds, were unworthy.

Christina gnashed her teeth. "Martin does not have to—"

Her mother's eyebrows climbed to her hairline, and Christina silently cursed that slip.

Martin lingered a moment, and then she watched as he walked off, stealing the first spot of light she'd known and dousing her in darkness once more. The moment she'd gone, Christina wheeled on her mother. "How dare you treat—?"

"How dare I?" her mother raged. "How dare you?" She lowered her voice. "Throwing yourself at that man so," she hissed.

"I was not throwing myself at him," she said firmly, and she hadn't. She and Martin had more moved toward each other.

"Bah," her mother exclaimed. "It wasn't enough that I let you marry an impoverished member of the gentry—"

She sputtered, but her mother raised her voice, continuing her tirade over Christina's outraged exclamations.

"I advised you against marrying him. I said he would leave you penniless and strip you of your pride and shame in his failure to provide, and I was correct."

Heat filled her cheeks and covered her chest and neck and the whole of her body. "How dare you speak of him so?" she hissed.

"I'm not speaking of him. I'm speaking of you and your actions," her mother shot back. "Before, you'd only had yourself and your future children to think of. Well, now you have four actual children. As such, I would advise that you *cease* throwing yourself at some man, like any other wanton widow, and remember those responsibilities and—"

Her eye caught a faint movement at the doorway. "Lachlan!" she said, her voice slightly squeaky. "How are you?"

That managed to silence Christina's mother as she turned and looked squarely at the little boy.

The little boy with suspicion enough in his eyes for a grown man.

He thinned his eyes and moved that suspicious gaze between his mother and grandmother and back to his mother.

"What's going on?" he asked, ignoring her greeting.

The dowager baroness, as absent of maternal affection as she was grandmotherly, frowned. "Children respect their elders and do not pose questions to them," she said coolly and managed to penetrate Lachlan's suspicion. He swiftly lowered his head, turning his eyes to the floor.

A moment later, the remainder of Christina's children came racing in, their governess trailing close at their heels.

Christina frowned and looked about. "Where is Lara?"

Just as Lachlan had done before, the nursemaid dipped her gaze. "I advised that she remain behind with her nursemaid." Her lips tightened. "It is… better this way."

Better as in it was hard enough catching a husband with three children, but to do so with a babe was nigh impossible. Or it would be. There was no doubting this guest list had been curated with a careful consideration of those who'd be willing to overlook Christina's impoverished state and the number of children she'd bring to a second marriage.

As if on cue, several guests entered, all gentlemen, all older in age, all bachelors or widowers, and, more, all in the market for a wife.

And she felt an overwhelming urge to weep, her morosity matching that of her sullen-for-them children.

"Put a smile on your face this instant," her mother ordered in a barely there whisper from the corner of her mouth.

Put a smile on your face.

It was what she'd made herself do these past years since her husband's illness and passing. Always smiling, for others.

Christina donned an empty-feeling smile and set to work creating the arrangements with her children and the guests who'd joined them.

All the while wishing another was here instead.

Chapter 12

It'd been two nights since Martin had arrived. He'd been certain he would be miserable at the posh affair hosted by a lady of the peerage and surrounded by her equally powerful friends and family.

He'd been wrong.

About any number of things.

He'd had a surprisingly deuced good time.

Though, in fairness, it wasn't the affair so much as the company.

"But *I* want to be the piggy." That little wail went up around the parlor.

Martin felt a smile form as Luna stamped her foot and proceeded to make an impressive argument as to why she should be the farmer and not her eldest brother, who was being spun about three times by Christina's sister and the hostess, Mrs. Gray.

All around them, the guests continued with the gameplay over the noisy interruption.

Christina bent over, speaking animatedly to the girl. With a belligerent tilt to her features, the lady's daughter folded her arms and shook her head. The pair continued talking while the parlor game continued.

And he stared on. The mothers of her status whom he'd observed while working in those fine households didn't bother with their children. They left those tasks to the nursemaids and governesses, and when they did have guests to gather, they kept those children out of sight.

"She reminds me of Alice."

Martin started and looked over at his brother, whose presence he'd failed to register, but who had registered where Martin's attention was directed.

Thad gave a slight nod, gesturing across the room, and Martin followed that discreet point to the guests seated in a large circle on the Aubusson carpet.

He exhaled a silent sigh of relief that his brother had mistaken his central focus that moment as being on the child, not the mother.

"She does," he agreed. That much was true. Mischievous, spirited, and bold as the English day was hard, Luna reminded him in so many ways of his sister who'd passed away.

"You aren't playing?"

"No." He was keeping his distance from Christina. Because that was for the best. The lady had to find a husband, one who was certainly not a mere builder from East London. Not that he, as a builder from East London, had the time for a wife.

Why was he not so convinced by that last part?

"Squeak, piggy, squeak!" Lachlan shouted as he planted himself on the latest challenger's lap.

Tynan Wylie, big former jailer, gave a high-pitched squeal, and everyone around the room roared with laughter.

Everyone except Christina and Luna, who'd now taken up place in the opposite corner of the room. Mother and daughter were still locked in a discussion. Luna jutted her lower lip out and folded her arms. The little girl shook her head mutinously.

"I'm going to see if I can help," Thad said.

Help Christina with Luna? Martin should let him go. He should let his younger, more affable brother join the pair, while Martin continued to keep his distance. That was safer and wiser, and yet—

"I'll go!" he said quickly when his brother made to leave.

Thad turned and gave him a quizzical look.

Martin gave thanks for the low glow provided by the candlelight, for it surely concealed a telltale flush. He cleared his throat and feigned casualness. "That is, given I've had more exchanges with"—Christina—"the family."

His brother slanted another probing glance his way. "Of course. That makes… sense."

Despite the wry twist to that acknowledgment, Martin hastened off, cutting a wide path around the latest game of squeak piggy squeak unfolding, with Tynan Wylie having moved into the role of the one guessing the identities of the little piggies around him.

As Martin drew upon them, the plaintive words of Christina's daughter reached him. "I neevvvver get to be a piggyyyyy," Luna was lamenting.

"*Of course* you do," Christina said, her response rich with exasperation. "We've played this numerous times with your cousins and—"

"Never the grownups," Luna railed, stamping her foot.

"This is different."

"It isn't."

"I don't know about previous games," Martin said, raising his voice a notch to be heard over the spiraling debate growing between mother and daughter.

The pair instantly stopped quarreling and looked his way.

The defiant glimmer in Luna's eyes went out in an instant. "Martin!" she cried happily, and he felt a rush of warmth at that clear joy at his presence from the little girl, who in a short time had managed to weave her way into his heart.

Her smile fell. "They won't let me play. Lachlan gets to play."

"Logan does not," Christina interjected that reminder for her daughter.

"Logan didn't want to," Luna shot back, and mother and child proceeded to raise their voices at each other in a bid to be heard.

"I suspect I know why Logan didn't want to and certainly why your mother doesn't want you to." He dangled that loudly enough to penetrate the noisy din of the room and the fight between Christina and Luna.

Luna's brow wrinkled. "You do?"

He stepped aside so the parlor game taking place was on full display for the little girl. "It's just that Tynan Wylie and your other uncles strike me as big men, and if you're on the floor, and they go sitting on your lap, they're going to squish you good."

Luna giggled. "Are you making a jest?"

As perfectly timed to the talk Martin was having with the girl, Tynan Wylie landed on the lap of a tiny slip of a woman, whom Martin had been introduced to a day earlier as Wylie's wife and Christina's sister.

Faye Wylie's squeal was a cross between a boisterous laugh and a groan.

"Does it look like I'm making a jest?" he said with a grin.

Luna smiled more widely. "No."

Martin nodded once. "Exactly. Just be thankful you don't have one of your big uncles, or me, going around sitting on your lap, squishing *you*."

The little girl giggled again.

Christina caught his gaze. "Thank you," she mouthed over the top of Luna's head.

He inclined his head in a silent acknowledgment, and in that instant, the room melted away as they partook in an exchange between only the two of them, her eyes locked with Martin's and his with hers. When they two were together, he could imagine a bucolic life for himself. It was a future and vision he'd not allowed himself, the sole reason being his work consumed him and hadn't allowed him to have thoughts of anything more, certainly not about a personal life and family.

Small pandemonium ensued in the form of guests laughing and trading places on the floor as the present came rushing back like a massive roar in his ears. In the middle of the room, Faye Wylie was blindfolded in preparation for the next match.

"Very well. I do not want to get squished, especially by Uncle Caleb," Luna conceded, pointing at the big American seated between his wife and Christina's brother, Tristan, the Baron of Bolingbroke.

"Clever girl." Martin winked at Christina's daughter.

"But why must we stay here and watch if I can't play?" Luna asked, and before they could answer, she caught first Christina and then Martin by the hand and gave a firm tug.

He and Christina's gazes held once more.

They shouldn't leave.

Nothing good could come from being alone with her anymore.

And yet...

"Well, come on, then," Luna said exasperatedly and gave another impressive pull, leading them onward.

The moment they left the parlor, the revelry within faded and grew distant, until it was gone altogether. Luna then freed their hands and went skipping on through the halls. Her little legs carried her several paces ahead, leaving Martin and Christina trailing after her.

"Thank you for that," Christina said when they were alone. "For distracting her from what was going to become a very public scene and for letting her pull you away from the festivities."

Pull him away? That statement suggested he would have preferred to stay in the room he'd just quit and not be here alone with her. He waved his hand. "I was happy to."

Color splashed the lady's cheeks. "My mother was unpardonably rude. She is... something of a vile person, and I'm sorry you were subjected to her disapproval."

"You don't have to make apologies for your mother, Christina. Her actions are her own."

"If it is any consolation, she is as disapproving toward me and my children and her other children and grandchildren and really anyone."

What a miserable parent to have had growing up. Martin's family had known financial struggles, but his ma and da had only ever showered him and his siblings with warmth and love. Despite that, Christina had emerged as a doting, playful, and loving mama.

Up ahead, Luna sang as loudly as she surely could a song in a roughened child's version of German.

Stille Nacht, heilige Nacht,
Alles schläft; einsam wacht
Nur das traute hochheilige Paar.

"You're wondering how I turned out differently than my mother," Christina rightly predicted, sliding him a look.

"I'm wondering how such a person could have a child so different than herself," he amended, watching the small girl singing up ahead.

As they walked, the soft swish of her satin skirts occasionally peeked through her daughter's boisterous carol. The faded sapphire material brushed Martin's leg in what should have been a perfectly innocuous meeting of his thigh and her dress, and yet, he might as well have been a green boy for the dizzying effect it had.

"When I was a girl," Christina began softly, "I felt constantly on needles. Worrying about how I walked or talked before her. Waiting for the inevitable times she'd attack me for being unladylike."

Up ahead, Luna zigzagged across the floors, singing

Christmas carols at the top of her lungs.

"When I was about eight or so, she observed one of my singing lessons and proceeded to berate me for sounding too happy when I sang."

Too happy?

As if a sad juxtaposition of the story she now shared, her daughter's happy-tinged song wafted back to meet them.

> *Stille Nacht, heilige Nacht,*
> *Hirten erst kundgemacht*
> *Durch der Engel Halleluja,*
> *Tönt es laut von fern und nah:*
> *Christ, der Retter ist da!*
> *Christ, der Retter ist da!*

Pain squeezed his heart.

Being hungry and struggling as he and his family had, Martin had always assumed the lives of the peerage were comfortable and easy in every way. He'd failed to consider all the ways in which his life had been full compared to those same fortunate lords and ladies. And he hated that she'd known unkindness from the people who were supposed to love her the most.

"And that was when I knew," Christina said softly, drawing his gaze to hers once more.

They stopped outside the door to the music parlor. "Knew?"

"I knew that if and when I had children of my own, I'd only ever want them to be happy. I knew I'd let them sing and dance and play without being shamed for feeling and showing joy."

He skimmed his eyes over the delicate planes of her lightly freckled face. "You are an amazing woman, Christina," he said quietly.

A sad smile creased the lines of her mouth. "If I were amazing, I would be able to care for myself and my children and not be putting myself on display to catch a husband for security, not love."

"The fact that you aren't able isn't a reflection on you. It's simply the world we live in."

She bit hard on her lip. "Thank you."

"I haven't done anything but speak the truth."

"I've spent so many months hating myself for having to make an emotionless match. It's mercenary. It's ugly." She hugged herself. "It's… necessary."

His eyes slipped to her mouth, that same mouth he'd taken under his and which consumed his thoughts day and night, still.

And he suspected he always might feel that way.

Because a man didn't kiss a mouth like that and remain the same afterward.

"Mama! Martin!" As one, they snapped their attention toward Luna.

The little girl giggled and pointed up.

They followed that little digit.

The crisp green sprigs tied with a bright red bow stared down.

"*Mistletoooooe*," Luna said. "Uncle Tristan told Aunt Poppy that whenever they stand under it, they must *kisssss*." The girl's face puckered as if she'd been grossed out by her own suggestion. And then Luna tossed her arms up. "I don't make the mistletoe rules."

Martin hesitated, and Christina dampened her mouth, highlighting her lips.

Forgoing the kind of kiss he would forever crave long after he left this place, he gathered her wrist in his, raising it to his lips. And then he placed a slow, gentle kiss upon that place where the inside of her wrist met her hand. All the while, their eyes remained locked, and he lingered there in that delicate kiss, unable to release her or this moment—

"Martin, you are sooooo smart!"

As if burned, he released Christina, and her arm fell swiftly to her side.

"You don't have to have one of those yuuucky kisses! You found a way around it."

Clapping excitedly, Luna bolted into the music room and resumed singing at the top of her lungs.

> *Stille Nacht, heilige Nacht,*
> *Gottes Sohn, o wie lacht*
> *Lieb' aus deinem göttlichen Mund,*
> *Da uns schlägt die rettende Stund'.*
> *Christ, in deiner Geburt!*
> *Christ, in deiner Geburt!*

Christina entered after her daughter, seating herself at the second row of chairs that had been set up, while Luna settled herself at the pianoforte. As she sang, the little girl brought her tiny fingers down harshly, playing an endearingly boisterous and crude melody that was slightly too slow for the speed with which she belted out the lyrics.

Martin should leave the pair alone.

He wasn't long for this family or this place.

Except…

Christina angled a glance over her shoulder, lifting her brow in question. In invitation.

Martin found himself unable to care about what he should or should not do, unable to resist the pull and the desire to be in this moment with her.

Of their own volition, his legs carried him over, and he settled onto a gilded side chair just as Luna finished her song.

The girl jumped up and sketched a deep, dramatic bow.

Together, Martin and Christina broke into applause.

Putting his two middle fingers in his mouth, he whistled his approval.

Instead of the horror he'd expect to be greeted with by most ladies, Christina matched his movements and whistled even louder and more wildly, and he laughed.

Laughed as he'd not laughed in more years than he could remember, because as a working man married to his craft, there weren't opportunities for revelry and playful moments. There were responsibilities and design plans and clients to meet with.

In short, there weren't opportunities for light moments like this because he didn't allow himself to have them.

Cupping her hands around her mouth, Christina called out, "Encore! Encore!"

Luna promptly hopped onto the bench and launched into a song from the Psalms of David.

Joy to the World; the Lord is come!
Let earth receive her King!

"Why must you have an emotionless match?" he asked quietly, while the little girl played a boisterous round of the lyrics by English writer Isaac Watts. "Why can you not find happiness with someone who is going to make you happy? Why does it have to be emotionless?"

Let ev'ry heart prepare Him room,
And Heaven and nature sing.

"Have you *seen* the men my mother invited, Martin?" she asked, lifting her focus from Luna fully engrossed at the keyboard.

Yes, he had.

Joy to the earth, the Saviour reigns!
Let men their songs employ;

"We made floral arrangements, and one gentleman continually checked his fob, and not at all discreetly. Another calls Luna *Lana*. Only one of them is taking part in the parlor games, and even *he* did so only because his *mother* insisted, and none too quietly. Do those strike you as men whom I can be happy with?"

While fields and floods, rocks, hills and plains
Repeat the sounding joy.

As they fell silent, listening to Luna's rendition of that Christian psalm, Martin considered Christina's words. The men she'd spoken of, the same ones he'd observed, were a bunch of dullards undeserving of the young woman and her children. And the idea of her with them made Martin want to growl and scare those pathetic dandies, those sorry excuses of men away.

No, Christina deserved a man who appreciated her wit and who could marvel at her knowledge when it came to design aesthetics. One who encouraged her to pursue her passions and didn't seek to quash them. He'd known Christina Thacker only a short time, and he'd come to care enough about the feisty lady to know he wanted that for her, and that she deserved it.

He glanced down at Christina, her focus forward on her daughter, her lips moving in time to the somewhat halting but exuberant song.

As if she felt his stare, Christina looked up. Her eyes slid a path over his face. "What is it?" she asked softly.

"You got dealt a shite hand in life, Christina. To have lost your love and been left alone, trying to navigate with four children, is the height of unfair." He leaned down, holding her stare. "And it'd be a damned shame and a crime if instead of again finding the happiness you are so deserving of, you consigned yourself to an empty union with some chap who isn't worthy of you or your children."

The lady's breath caught, her chest hitching slightly. Then a sudden rush of sadness stole away the brief glimmer of light in her expressive eyes.

"Did they put a timetable on it?" he asked. "Is your family's support contingent upon you making a match during these ten or so days here?"

"No."

"Would they ever rush you into a match to be free of you and your children?" he asked, even as he knew the answer. Knew because he'd witnessed her closeness with her siblings.

"No," she said instantly. "They would never."

"Then as I see it…there's nothing saying you have your future decided by the end of this house party."

With that, he directed his attention to the little girl rushing quickly through the last of those lyrics.

> *He rules the world with truth and grace,*
> *And makes the nations prove*
> *The glories of His righteousness,*
> *And wonders of His love.*

The moment she'd concluded, Martin exploded from his seat, clapping wildly and stamping his left foot.

As Luna beamed and darted to her feet, sketching bow after deep bow, Martin caught a glimpse of Christina from the corner of his eye as she stood. She was watching him. And he felt her as she shifted closer to him, standing so near that their legs brushed.

Then, as Luna hopped onto the bench and proceeded to sing a third carol, Christina slid her fingers into his, twining her soft, long digits with his coarse, longer ones.

Chapter 13

Christina knew she was supposed to be fixed on finding a husband.

She knew, without her mother's unnecessary reminders, precisely what was needed of her, especially as a mother with four children.

After all, a young, penniless widow with two young sons and two even younger daughters didn't have the luxury of even a minute to forget that those same little souls whom she loved with every corner of her heart relied upon her now for their complete and total security.

And yet, in the following days of her sister's house party, even knowing she had to wed, she'd also decided Martin was correct. While she'd been seated beside him, listening to Luna's solo Christmas music concert, his words had reached deep inside, seducing her with the idea that she might steal joy for herself.

Eventually, she would do that which she needed to do for her family.

But for now, she was determined to find a brief window of happiness for herself.

Though, in truth, it wasn't just for her.

In the courtyard, the peals of her children's excited

squeals filled the air as they darted among the stone pillars. Lachlan and Logan and Luna were engaged in an intense snowball battle with Martin and his brother.

Logan hurled a snowball, and it sailed past Martin's broad shoulder, and he and his brother took off running, hiding once more. Cradling Lara, wrapped in a fur blanket, Christina watched on.

When had her children last laughed so?

When had she last smiled so?

Absently, she alternately bounced the baby lightly up and down and shifted back and forth as her youngest daughter fiddled with Christina's necklace.

She'd been sad for so long that she'd believed there could never be happiness again.

Only to have found more joy in more years than she could recall.

"Ball, ball, ball," Lara babbled, pumping a chubby fist in the air as if attempting to join in the snow fight unfolding across the courtyard.

"Oh, you will have plenty of time in the future to play in such games," she promised. Alas, during the time Martin had been visiting here for the holiday party, he'd taken care to include Lara in all the games as he was able. Even if it had been to just hold her in the middle of whatever melee, he, her children, and his brother had been engaged in.

"Pla, pla, pla."

"Later, you can play," she promised. "When it is a safer game."

"Ya, ya, ya," her youngest daughter squealed happily.

Only, as Christina cradled her closer and stared on at the

happy scene before them, Martin and Thaddeus both taking cover and her children doing the same, she wondered whether she could truly make such a promise.

Five days earlier, when he'd said women's place in the world was an unfair and uncertain one, Martin had spoken *all* the truths. The moment a woman wed, she, along with her children, became the property of another. And what if the man she did end up having to wed took umbrage with her children's antics?

Her breathing grew panicky, the tufts of white she swiftly exhaled forming a cloudlike halo over Lara's deep hood.

What if the man she ultimately settled on sought to curtail their games and—

"There you are!"

She gasped and spun around.

Her youngest daughter released a squeal of excitement at the sudden turn.

Her younger sisters, in matching crimson cloaks, stared oddly back.

"Claire," she said weakly, greeting her siblings. "Faye."

"No need to sound so glum," Claire said wryly and rubbed her gloved fingers together.

"Fa, Fa, Fa," Lara cooed, reaching for her aunt.

"Not all are unhappy to see us," Faye murmured, extending her arms for the tiny babe who'd always had a close bond with the youngest of Christina's siblings. As she made to hand her daughter over, Lara all but dove for the other woman. Faye snuggled her close, burying her head in the crook of her shoulder and nuzzling the babe, earning breathless little giggles from Christina's babe. "It is not as though *Mother* came upon you," Faye added in her tones that were equal parts eerie and enchanting.

"Forgive me, I was just surprised. And lost in my head…" Christina murmured that afterthought as she turned to the courtyard that had gone quiet. There was a lull in the fight as both sides regrouped, and she peered at the pillar Martin where had made his shelter.

Who would have imagined that after their first volatile meeting and the quarrel between he and her children, he'd be even now engaging in games with them? And that she'd be more comfortable in speaking to him about secrets she carried than anyone?

Claire rested a hand upon her shoulder, startling her out of her thoughts. "I'm so sorry," her younger sister said. "I cannot imagine the pain of your loss."

The pain of your loss. It was a familiar phrase that had been spoken to Christina by so many people offering their condolences after her husband's death. And that was what had consumed her. As such, it was the correct assumption for her younger sister to make. Christina had been grieving and filled with sorrow over the loss of her husband for so long that one would expect it had been her departed spouse who'd occupied her thoughts just now.

Only, this time, he wasn't the reason for her sadness. Somewhere along the way, she'd learned to smile again. And now she found herself mourning something she was afraid to put her finger on. Something… surrounding the man now at play with her children.

"Every day, I hope it will get better for you," Claire went on when Christina failed to say anything, because really, what was there to say? "Because no one deserves happiness more than you."

Faye murmured her ascent.

I respect the fact that you have others whose care you're reliant upon. I just don't want you to fail to acknowledge what you deserve and want: You enjoy designing interiors. You have vision. You deserve to pursue that if you wish. You deserve to be happy, Christina. Whatever will bring you joy…

"It has gotten better," she murmured, her gaze still on the pillar Martin hid behind. A wintry breeze rolled across the landscape, stirring little flakes of snow that had not been cleared from the stone terrace. And she was stunned even as the admission left her that those were words she could say. And this time, for the *first* time in so long, she actually meant them.

Feeling her sisters' eyes upon her, she glanced over. Their expressions were hesitant, their gazes filled with suitable disbelief, given the constant cloud of sadness that had followed Christina these years.

"It has," she insisted, looking off to where Martin, his brother, and Christina's children remained in hiding. "I'm just in a different state of mourning," she confessed. Because if one could not be honest with one's sisters, then whom could one be honest with?

Faye touched her other shoulder the way Claire had. "You know you do not have to marry again. None of us would ever force it or expect it."

No, but she'd expect it of herself. It was one thing being a poor relation dependent upon the generosity of her siblings. It was an altogether different matter having four children and expecting her siblings and their spouses to see to them indefinitely. "But I do," she murmured. "There will be Eton and Cambridge for the boys and Seasons for the girls, trousseaus and doweries." There would be no end to the expenses.

"But those aren't reasons to marry," Claire insisted, and Faye nodded her agreement. Lara bounced up and down boisterously, adding her support to her aunts'. "You deserve love, and you are young enough to have that again, Christina."

There would have been a time when she would have shot a question at her so assured sisters, when she would have asked if she or Faye could see themselves wedding again if something were to happen to Caleb or Tynan.

This time, however, that assertion of the fact that she'd already loved and never would again did not come.

Some twenty paces away, Martin darted out from behind his pillar with a war whoop. Finding her children's hiding spot, he and his brother converged upon the three children, pelting them lightly with snowballs.

Logan, Lachlan, and Luna came racing out from their hiding place, laughing and shouting as they did.

Claire's eyebrows lifted slightly as she looked from Christina to Martin and back again. But then, whatever knowing glint Christina thought she saw was gone so quickly she expected it had been her own sentiments that had accounted for that speculation.

"Misters Phippen are quite good with them," Claire remarked, and once again, Christina attempted to search for the hint of more within that innocuous statement. But she found none.

"Yes, they are," she said, her eyes capable of seeing just one of those two powerful men.

Luna launched a snowball with all her might, and it landed with a soft splatter against Martin's broad chest.

With an overdramatic groan, as if he'd taken an arrow to the chest, Martin tossed his arms wide and staggered back several steps. Then, coming down to his knees, he keeled over sideways.

"Woo-hoo! I have defeated him," Luna cried, throwing her joined fists in the air and waving them victoriously.

"*We* have," Logan corrected. "We are a teeeeam. Plus, there is still Mr. Thad."

Only, as the trio turned their sights on Thaddeus, Martin slowly sat upright. Forming two snowballs, he caught the unsuspecting brothers between their shoulder blades.

A laugh exploded from Christina, and her frame shook. The exhalation of her mirth filled the air with a cloud of white.

Again, her sisters probed her with their stares, and Christina resisted the urge to squirm. "It is just so very good to see them laugh again."

"I can agree with that," Claire murmured.

"We all can," Faye said. "And especially when having fun seemed doubtful upon your arrival, with mother having you under her fist."

"Which brings me to the reason I sought you out," Claire said.

Christina flashed a questioning glance at her.

"Mother was looking for you. She is hoping you'd join

her and... several other guests."

Hoping? The dowager baroness asked for nothing. She either took what she wished or insisted it be given to her as though it were her due.

Christina groaned.

"We thought we might help," Claire said.

Neither her sisters could even if they wanted to, and she knew they did. "When Mother has something in her head, there is no deterring her," she muttered. "Who is he?"

Claire and Faye exchanged a look.

"Lady Milwheate and her son, Lord Thomas," Faye said.

"Lord Thomas intends to read Christmas stories, and as such, she asked that the children come along for the reading."

The tall, lanky gentleman was nice enough and likely would have been a good enough match if he weren't a mother's boy who insisted on having the stern lady about for all their exchanges.

Christina groaned.

"Those were our sentiments exactly," Faye murmured in commiserative tones.

"Which is why we told her that we'd already enlisted you to collect more greenery for the additional mistletoe we need." With that, Claire reached inside the pocket of her cloak and withdrew a pair of scissors.

Christina made a grab for the gleaming silver articles.

Shifting Lara so she was balanced on one hip, Faye reached for a wicker basket beside her feet that Christina had until now failed to notice.

"What would I do without you?" she asked, tears gleaming.

"Oh, do stop," Claire urged, catching Christina in a loose hug. "None of that."

"Tears are good," Faye murmured in her haunting tones, earning a smile from both sisters. "They are cathartic and quite wonderful."

Christina could attest to that affirmation from her youngest sibling.

"Nor, for that matter, shall you ever have to find out what you would do without us," Claire promised, and then catching Logan's attention, she waved her arms. "Grandmother asked that I fetch you," she called out, interrupting the play and heading over to the melee.

As one, the children promptly ceased their snow fight.

"She is looking for you." Claire spoke over the collective groans of Lachlan, Logan, and Luna. "*Which* is why I thought you might rather come along and join in a game of hide-and-seek with your cousins?"

Christina's children promptly charged their aunt, throwing their arms about her.

Laughing exuberantly, she folded the trio into an awkward hug. "Mr. Phippen, Mr. Phippen," she said over the tops of their heads, "I am sorry to rip you away from your play."

Martin tipped his hat. "You've done us a favor, ma'am, as we were about to be ambushed and suffer a devastating defeat."

"This isn't over," Lachlan shouted, pointing a finger at Martin. The playful way he waggled his finger and the glimmer in his eyes, however, bespoke the teasing nature of his vow.

Martin and Thaddeus folded their arms in a matching way. "It isn't," they promised as one.

Thaddeus leaned in. "We're going to regroup."

"Alas..." Claire interrupted the light repartee between the adults and children embroiled in their rivalry. "I fear your strategizing session must wait, Mr. Phippen," she said to Thad. "I was thinking you might take on one of the hide-and-seek teams with Tynan and that, Mr. Phippen"—she looked to Martin—"you might help my sister with some greenery I require." With that, she fished a second pair of scissors out of her cloak and handed them over.

Chapter 14

Quiet.

It hung like a blanket over the rolling, snow-covered grounds of the Yorkshire countryside.

There was only the occasional whistle of the winter wind as it issued a plaintive, mournful cry.

Christina had come to hate the quiet. When Patrick had taken ill, she had instructed her children to maintain a silent state so that he might sleep. Not that she'd needed to issue any orders. There'd been an unnatural somberness and quiet that had descended over their modest home. Their sadness and fear of their father's sickness had resulted in an adherence to the calm.

Or she'd thought she hated the quiet.

Now, walking alongside Martin, the two of them perusing her sister's barren gardens, she found a natural ease to the silence that came just from being with him.

She didn't have to force conversation.

The quiet between them was as natural as the discourse that came so freely.

"More greenery?" he asked as they walked. In his left hand, he swung the basket. "Is she determined to have mistletoe over every doorway?"

Her lips twitched, until she recalled the real reason for this excursion. "More like we're playing our own game of hide-and-seek," she mumbled under her breath, assessing her sister's gardens, largely dead and barren for the winter with the exception of the yew, box, holly, and mistletoe, evergreens and bushes suited for harsh weather.

Martin looked at her questioningly.

"She selected a gentleman," she said.

When he continued to stare confusedly back, she elucidated. "My mother. She's searching for me because she's found a gentleman who doesn't mind my impoverished state." With every word that left her lips, her steps became more frantic. "Or taking on my four children and seeing to the care of five additional mouths." She abruptly stopped and stared forlornly off at the red berries of a holly bush in the distance.

She should be grateful. She should be relieved.

Why, then, did she want to dissolve into the snow and sob like a babe?

"Which fellow?"

Christina started and, blinking several times, looked up at Martin.

"He's not... terrible. Lord Thomas," she muttered.

"The mama's boy?"

Her lips twitched again. "You noticed that?"

"I'm sure everyone has noticed. She cut his lamb at last night's supper," he drawled, and Christina burst into a pained laugh. Catching Martin's hand, she buried her head against his shoulder.

Their laughter melded, and then, as the moment faded,

he brushed back her hood, exposing her gaze to his.

He touched a stray curl that hung over her brow, tucking it back behind her ear. "And is that what you want? Someone who is not terrible?"

"No," she said instantly, that answer coming with a confidence that hadn't been there before this man. He'd helped her to see that.

He squeezed her hand. "Good. What do you want?"

You. I want… you.

She'd expect the truth of that should have bowled her over.

Falling in love for a second time, and doing so with a man whom she'd known less than ten days, should have shocked and mayhap even horrified her.

Only, it didn't.

She knew better than anyone how fickle and transient life and happiness were, and as such, she knew just how important it was to take her joy when it presented itself.

His gaze darkened, and his eyebrows dipped. "Christina?" he asked.

"What do you want?" she countered.

He stared blankly back.

"It's just, you ask me about what I want for my future and encourage me to find that which makes me happy, and you even know what does." It was an interest they shared and one she'd revealed to no one, for the simple reason that mothers—widowed ones, at that—hardly had the time for their own happiness. "But I don't know those things about you." He opened his mouth. "I know you love your work," she went on. "I know you love your family." His easygoing and warm relationship with his brother bespoke a man devoted. "But what do you want of life?" It wasn't merely an evasive response. She desperately ached and yearned to know about him and his dreams.

He remained silent, and she would wager this hesitant, more than slightly perplexed look to him had been the same one she had worn when he had asked that question of her.

Finally, Martin lifted his gloved palms. His leather gloves were intact and functional, but also not the high-quality, fine fabric worn by the other guests. "I... I've always just worked." There was a wistful nature to that admission. "My family has always been of humble origins. My da was a bricklayer. And all my siblings and I started out doing the harshest, hardest jobs, and maybe that is why I've always been driven to be the best. When I was a boy, I wanted to design and build to prove a person didn't have to be born in your craft to be the best at it. As such, this, the life I'm living, was an even grander dream than I could've ever imagined." His voice grew more impassioned as he spoke. "Having anything of my own, having men and women who carry out the visions I draw up..." He'd become something more than anyone raised in East London could expect or even hope for. "But I've always been so consumed with my work that I didn't dream beyond the dream." As if recalling her presence, he looked down. "Does that make sense?"

She nodded. "It does," she said softly. So much admiration for this man swept through her. For what he had accomplished through his hard work and his own efforts. Everything Martin had attained was not because of what had been handed to him or who he had known. Rather, he had built himself up. He had risen from the ashes of an unfair life and blazed bright as one of the most successful and sought-after master builders in London. Christina shifted closer and craned her neck back a fraction to meet his gaze. "But of anyone who is deserving of dreams beyond work, Martin, it is you. A man who's done backbreaking work the whole of his life to establish a future, one that has seen you not only successful but able to care for your siblings."

Their stares locked, and then, as naturally as though they'd known each other the whole of their lives, their hands came up in tandem, their fingers twining together.

She lightly squeezed his fingertips. Or mayhap the two of them moved in unison in that, too.

In that moment, Christina let herself acknowledge the whole truth—she wanted him. He was a bachelor and married to his business, and he'd shown no interest in a greater commitment for more. By even his own revelations just now, he had anything but a wife and four babes on his mind.

"What is it?" he murmured, stroking her cheek with his other palm, and she leaned into his touch.

She shook her head slightly, unable to speak those specific truths to him. Her pride prevented it. Common sense also. "I'm just... happy." She settled for different truths instead. "It feels so very good having someone to speak honestly with."

"I want you to have that forever, Christina," he said simply. "You deserve that."

She wanted to have that with him.

She knew falling in love was unlikely. Doing so twice

would be like capturing lightning in a bottle.

His expression darkened, and she knew he would kiss her even before he lowered his head, because in their brief time together, she'd grown accustomed to the nuances of his thoughts and his actions. She tipped her head back to receive his kiss.

A soft sigh slipped from her lips just as he covered them with his own in a tender kiss that threatened to break her and, in a deepening embrace, promised to put her back together.

He caught her by the waist, drawing her into his arms, and she moaned, melting against him.

Martin kissed her, making love to it in ways she'd not known lips could be loved. He tasted and teased and nipped, and standing outside as they were, not even the winter's chill could penetrate the heat of his embrace.

Christina wound her hands about his neck and pressed herself closer, wanting to climb inside him and take the forever with him that she wished. Such a revelation would only send him running.

She pushed back those unwelcome thoughts, sobering ones that threatened to steal this moment from her. She'd surrender enough in the coming days that she'd not let this be one of those moments, too.

Martin kissed the right corner of her mouth and moved his worship lower. Burying his head in the crook of her shoulder, knocking her hood back, he availed himself of the sensitive skin of her neck.

Christina whimpered, catching his arms hard, gripping him tightly and clinging as he continued to nip and lick. Nip and lick. And then he breathed softly upon that heated skin, the warmth of his breath a glorious juxtaposition to the winter's cold, and that sharp ache between her thighs grew sharper.

Suddenly, Martin caught her nape firmly, and this time when he covered her mouth with his, he devoured. There was nothing gentle or hesitant. His was a bold possession. He was a man laying siege, and she happily surrendered to him. Opening her mouth, she let Martin inside. He touched his tongue against hers in a bold, insistent slash. And she met every glide with her own.

Ping, ping, ping.

It came faintly.

The whir of desire filled her ears.

Ping, ping, ping, ping.

Her heart thumped against her chest…

Tap, tap, tap, tap.

Except…

She stilled in Martin's arms.

That tapping wasn't the rhythm of her wild heartbeat, a tempo that proved far quicker and more pounding.

She looked past him and looked up.

And dread settled in her belly. Dread and horror.

For lined up in the hall above were none other than her mother and three of her children; the eldest of whom was tapping his finger against the glass in a bid to gain Christina's attention.

Oh, no. No. No. No. This was *not* happening.

Just then, her mother slapped a palm over Luna's wide eyes.

Despite the many paces separating them, Christina caught the distinct formation of the words her mother spoke in that hall up above. "Now, Christina," the dowager baroness silently commanded, jabbing a spare finger toward the ground.

"Oh, hell," she whispered.

Chapter 15

Being discovered kissing a lady, by her mother and young children, was certainly enough to get any fellow tossed from the family's house party.

It was even more certain when the fellow doing the kissing was a commoner, as far out of his league with the people and lady present as a sinner sitting down to sup with his lord and savior.

As such, the sharp rapping on his chamber doors wasn't unexpected. Just the opposite.

"Oh, hell. We're getting the boot," his brother whispered, staring at the entry of Martin's guest chambers with the same horror he had when they'd been small, impish boys caught dipping their sisters' pigtails in ash to stain the ends.

"I would say that is a certainty," he muttered.

The question remained: Would it be the mother or the overprotective brother, who was well within his rights to thrash Martin? Or perhaps a servant had been sent to dispense them, rather than any of the distinguished family members.

Rap, rap, rap.

By the firm but polite knock, it seemed to suggest that it was decidedly not the brother or a brother-in-law, who might have been more likely to knock the door down to reach Martin.

"I expect you thought I would have my son toss you out, Mr. Phippen," the baroness said crisply, speaking his name like her tongue had been soured by simply having to address him so personally. "Or a servant perhaps?" she asked.

"I did wonder..."

"You see, I wouldn't." She began a slow turn around his room and then paused, eyeing his old trunk and valises. He had the funds enough to replace them, but hadn't seen a need to do so because they were still perfectly functional. Giving her head a disgusted shake, she looked back at him. "To do so would alert the distinguished guests present about what happened. It would result in a scene and a scandal, though not a hasty marriage, because"—she flicked a hand contemptibly at him—"of your station and all."

"Of course," he drawled, and by the way her brows dropped and her eyes narrowed, she'd detected the trace of insolence and likely didn't know what to do with such presumption from a man so beneath her.

She swiftly found herself. "More importantly, alerting the other guests would ruin the possibility of a match between my daughter and a good, honorable, respectable gentleman."

"Which I am not."

"Which you are clearly not," she said, raising her voice slightly for emphasis.

He stared at the coldhearted, ruthless lady before him. With her words and her actions and demeanor, her daughter bore no traces of this woman's soul. In fact, how did one such as the dowager baroness give birth to a devoted, loving mother and woman?

Christina's mother gave a slight toss of her head. "My daughter is a widow and was merely indulging in behaviors permitted a widow. You were fine enough for her to seek her pleasure with—"

"But not good enough to wed her?"

"Exactly," she confirmed with a brusque nod.

"Do you know what I think?"

"I really don't care what you—"

"You might not care, but you're going to hear it anyway," he said firmly over her interruption, his response eliciting a shocked gasp.

The dowager baroness fluttered a hand at her breast. "How dare you?"

"Quite easily."

"I can ruin you."

Fortunately, having spent almost two decades building his business and establishing himself, he wasn't a desperate young man reliant upon the mercy and kind word of one vengeful lady. There would have been a time in his career, back when he'd just begun, when a threat from a noblewoman would have elicited suitable fear, and he would have complied with anything so as to save his career. That wasn't now. "With all due respect, my business has been built, and my résumé is a respected one. I count dukes, earls, and viscounts among my clients. The opinions of peers I've actually worked *with*," he added that firm emphasis, "are going to be a far greater testament than any words from *you*." A viper who'd never employed him.

Color splotched her gaunt cheeks. "I've witnessed you here this past week." She scraped him over, giving him an up-and-down look. "You and your brother have been outrageous in your behaviors. Unrestrained. Impolite. Raucous. I want you gone, Mr. Phippen. The both of you. I want you and your brother both to take your hoydenish influence away from my grandchildren."

"And Christina?" he asked when she'd finished her stinging diatribe, deliberately using that beautiful first name and wringing another hideous flush of color from the old woman's cheeks.

"And from my daughter," she snapped and turned to make her grand exit.

For a minute, he almost pitied her. She *truly* believed she could stamp out the spirits of Luna, Lara, Logan, and Lachlan. She still didn't realize she hadn't managed as much with Christina, and she'd never accomplish such a feat with the young mother's offspring.

"And if I don't?" he called after her, and precise as she was with her steps, it was a moment before her steps slowed and stopped altogether. "What if I don't leave?" he clarified.

Slowly, Christina's mother turned back, facing him. "Why… you care for my daughter?" Surprise stamped her sharp features. It was an artful show, a careful arrangement of her face, as he expected everything with this woman was born of artifice.

"Would it matter if I did?" he asked, already knowing the answer before her nearly instantaneous reply.

"Of course not, Mr. Phippen." The dowager baroness took one step near him. "You see, I indulged my daughter's"—her lips puckered—"romantic heart once before. Against all better judgment, I conceded to a match between her and a man far beneath her—"

"A man she loved."

"A man she… loved." The older woman's lips pulled as if it had been a chore for the heartless dowager to wrap her mouth and mind around such an emotion. "I permitted it." Her gaze grew distant and far away. "Despite all attempts to reason with her, despite my best judgment, I allowed her to wed."

She might have given her reluctant blessing, but she'd not *allowed* anything. Christina had been young and without children whose happiness and futures she'd also had to consider, so Martin knew with an absolute definitiveness that she would have only followed her heart.

The dowager baroness gave her head a slight shake and returned to him and the moment. "You think I'm cruel," she remarked. "You find me controlling and heartless. I see it in your eyes, Mr. Phippen. But I did support Christina's union to that other man."

She couldn't even bring herself to breathe the poor, late fellow's name?

"I'd other daughters who would make a suitable match, and as such, I allowed myself that moment of weakness, one that went against all my better judgment. I freed Christina, who put herself first, while her sisters would carry out the responsibilities I expected of each of them."

She'd try to vilify Christina? It was all he could do to keep from delivering a heaping opinion of the other woman atop her head.

"How'd that work out for you?" he drawled, unable to resist baiting the shrew. "How did the whole expectations for Christina's sisters work out for you?" For in the end, each had wed self-made men.

The dowager baroness sucked in a sharp, shuddery breath through her teeth, and the cross between that sound and the small wart on the right corner of her nostril gave the lady a reptilianlike look. "I have indulged you long enough, Mr. Phippen. I lowered myself by coming here."

"You came because you're desperate to hide the fact that I was with your daughter." Embracing. They'd been embracing.

She sharpened her gaze on him. "And is that something you'd not keep secret?" she asked, sounding almost gleeful. "Would you happily ruin my daughter?"

No doubt she'd like to think that of him. "I wouldn't," Martin said icily. He'd sooner cut off his building arm with his dullest saw than deliberately hurt Christina Thacker. "And whatever lies you intend to head over to share with her, I trust *her* enough to know she won't believe a single one of them." And he did.

The dowager considered him for a long moment, assessing him, her study now a contemplative one. "You seem to genuinely care for my daughter," she began, in a clear attempt at trying a different approach. "You do not even seem to mind her children."

Mind them? "Her children are a joy," he said coolly, fighting the urge once more to dump every last ugly thought on the lady.

"Yes." She flicked an imagined fleck of dust from her

right puffed sleeve. "A joy, indeed. As I was saying, given that you truly appear to care for my daughter, I trust you also care about her future and those of her children."

As Christina's mother started to drone on, about him being an honorable man who'd surely do the honorable thing, his mind drifted. As wrong as the older woman was about so much, in this regard she'd proven spot-on. In his time with Christina, he'd come to care about both her *and* her children, those impish little ones with their enormous personalities and hearts. Between the five of them, they'd filled his work-centered, lonely life with laughter and happiness. They'd taught him to stop and smile and engage in games that he hadn't in years.

Nay, he didn't just *care* about them.

Martin stilled.

I love them…

Bowled over by that discovery, Martin jolted back as he fought to remain with his feet planted on the floor.

He loved Christina Thacker in all her spirit and passion for life. He loved that he'd come to find a woman who shared his interests, but had also proven to be someone whom he could speak with about all matters of life beyond his work.

"Mr. Phippen…" The dowager baroness' voice came as if from under water, muffled by the whirring in his ears and the pounding of his pulse in them. "Mr. Phippen," the dowager baroness repeated in a louder, shriller voice, bringing him rushing back to the present.

"Hmm?" Martin gave his head a slow, befuddled shake and forced himself to attend whatever it was she'd been saying in that moment.

Christina's mother stared expectantly. At him. "I trust you'll do the right thing?"

"The right thing," he repeated to her nod.

As in leave.

As in let her to some fine, fancy gent with not only the fortune that Martin could comfortably keep her and the children with, but who also came to the proverbial table with some old title.

Martin's hands formed automatic fists at his sides.

He loved her. He wanted the damned universe for the lady if she so wished it, because Lord knew, with the suffering she'd known and the strength and grace with which she'd come through all of that pain, that was the least of which she deserved.

Martin nodded slowly, reluctantly. "I'll do the right thing," he said quietly.

Christina's mother pressed a relieved hand to her heart, exhaling an audible sound of relief. "Thank you, Mr. Phippen. Thank you."

"Do not thank me." Martin didn't even attempt to hide his contempt and fury at her intercession. "As you pointed out, I care about Christina, and it's because of her that I'm doing this."

The lady lifted her head. "Good day, Mr. Phippen."

He expected she thought it was.

With that, the lady sailed off quickly, as if fearing he'd change his mind, and let herself out.

He stared at the closed panel.

There would have been a time when he'd have never

gone toe to toe with a powerful peeress. Not because he feared her empty threats of ruining his career, but because it wasn't worth it to spend his time with vipers of the peerage. Leaving, however, would also mean he wouldn't see Christina and that their time together would be at an end. Which was inevitable.

Both his departure and her eventual marriage.

The idea of her wedding one of those other fellows left him hollow inside.

Nay, there was only one thing left to do.

Chapter 16

Pfft, pfft. That loud squelching sound filled the quiet of Christina's otherwise silent bedchambers.

Those same chambers she'd sought in a rush after catching sight of her mother and three children watching on as she'd come undone in Martin's arms. Standing at the edge of the window, staring out at the gray skies and the light snow just beginning to fall, she tried to pretend none of the past hour had happened.

The thing of it was, before that interruption, it had been magical. There'd been fireworks to rival the ones she'd once watched in awe at Vauxhall Gardens. Great, bursting, white lights that had filled her belly and whole insides with the greatest warmth and happiness.

It should have remained only a moment of beauty and wonder, and it would have…

Had that intimate moment with Martin not been interrupted by an audience of not only her mother, but her three oldest children.

She cringed, certain there was no greater horror than being discovered by her own sons, daughter, and mother. Why, she'd have preferred being discovered by any of the strangers at her sister's affair.

At least the other guests would have simply chalked up her behavior as that of a wanton widow. Ultimately, the holiday party would come to an end, and those lords and ladies whom she barely knew, or knew not at all, would go their own ways, and she could go her own way and forget that she'd been spied in flagrante delicto.

No, instead, she'd be living out the remainder of her days with the ones who'd borne witness to her embrace with Martin.

Pffffffffft, pffffffffft.

"Would you quit that?" Logan muttered, tossing a pillow across the bed at Luna, who clutched one of the many silk throw pillows close.

"I'm kissing it. Like Mama was kissing—"

"That is enough," she squawked, spinning around and facing down three of her children, all old enough to know precisely what they'd seen. She stole a look at the doorway, more than half expecting one of her sister's guests to come pouring in to catch the remainder of that scandalous admission. "That is enough," she repeated in a quieter, more measured way meant to set the mood for what she needed from them.

"Why can't we talk about it?" Luna posed that question to the room at large.

"Because ladies don't go about kissing people," Logan whispered, his face pulling with all the distaste a boy of eight could feel. "Not that I'm sure why anyone would want to go about kissing Mama… or anyone."

"But whyyyy?" Luna persisted. "Mama seemed like she was having a good enough time with Martin."

Oh, God.

She burned with embarrassment. Fortunately, her eldest son still had his voice about him.

"We can't talk about it," Lachlan said in wooden tones. "Because Mama will be ruined and won't be able to make a match with one of the dandies present."

One of the dandies present. A man who was not Martin.

A moroseness descended over the room, a heavy blanket of sadness and silence.

"Well, I don't like the dandies present," Luna whispered. "I like Martin and Thaddeus. They aren't dandies, and Mama was kissing Martin, so he seems like the one she should—"

"Will you stop?" Lachlan tossed another pillow, catching Luna on the side of the head.

"Hey!" the little girl cried out.

"Will you both please stop?" Christina pleaded, and they must have heard something in her usually measured maternal tones, for all three children went absolutely silent.

Christina resisted the urge to press her fingertips against her temple to blot out the quarrel between her children and the image that would forever be stamped in her brain of being discovered by them. "We cannot speak of this, for the reasons Lachlan and Logan both provided. If it is discovered, people will say terrible things about me, and—"

"And I'll beat them good for it," Lachlan promised, punching his fist into his other hand in a way she expected would menace most grown men in the years to come.

"No one is beating anyone," she vowed. "No one. We cannot speak of this because people would speak poorly of me, and as a result you, and I'll not have anyone saying mean things about us."

"Because you have to marry a fancy fellow," Lachlan said bitterly.

Her heart physically hurt that he should be so aware of the dire way in which they found themselves. It meant she'd been unable to protect him, but it also meant he was now getting older, that he was no longer a small child unaware of life's cruelty.

"Because I don't want anyone judging me or Mr. Phippen or you," she said, holding her son's stare.

The boy glared and then looked off.

"We shall not speak of this to anyone."

"Not even Grandmother?" Luna asked.

Especially not Grandmother.

"Why would you want to speak to Grandmother about anything?" Lachlan asked in perplexed tones.

Luna's face scrunched up. "You're right. I don't."

Christina latched on to that. "Perfect. As you'd rather not speak to Grandmother, you'd certainly not wish to speak of anything that is going to be a topic that makes her angry."

"Even angrier, you mean." Lachlan sniggered, and Logan joined in laughing.

Yes, well at least they could find some reason to laugh for the day, and she was coward enough that she'd take any distraction on their part from thoughts of what they'd witnessed from the windows overhead.

"Now, why don't you go and find your cousins and resume your game of hide-and-seek?"

With no further prompting needed, Luna hopped off the

bed and scrambled over to the door. She stopped with her fingers on the handle and cast a suspicious glance over her shoulder. "You're sure Grandmother isn't going to find us and make us come with her again? She's ever so good at finding people."

Yes, she was.

"I can promise you she's not going to be looking for you." Not this time, anyway.

"How can you be *suuuuure*?" Luna asked. "She's always looking for us so she might parade us about and scold us and—"

"Because she's going to be looking for Mama," Lachlan interrupted. "That's why."

Luna beamed. "Splendid."

"Not for Mama," Lachlan added under his breath.

No, not for Mama. But Christina could take it. She could and would take any unpleasantness and misery for her children.

Was that really true, though? Would she make the match that her mother expected to see them settled?

Christina felt the sudden urge to cry, at finding herself trapped between what she wanted and what her children required. Because what she wanted... It wasn't really an actuality. It was a fantastical dream born of only her own wishing and hope. When life had taught her all the reasons to not trust in the ideas of faith and hope...

"Mama?" The hesitant query from Luna slashed across Christina's tortured musings. "Are you all right?"

She mustered a smile. "I'm fine. I was just... thinking of all the places you might hide from your cousins." Lachlan stared at Christina like the liar she was. "Run along," she urged her daughter.

Instantly reassured, as only a girl of five could be, Luna let herself out.

Logan hastened after his sister.

"Lachlan," Christina called when her other son followed along, albeit at a slower pace. "Will you remain a moment?"

The boy hesitated, and then, pushing the door closed, he faced her, his arms folded at his narrow chest.

Except, as she was now alone with him, she had absolutely no idea how to begin or what to say. "I… know you are likely upset."

"Yeah," he snapped. "I'm upset all right."

"Martin did not do anything which I—"

"I'm not angry with Martin."

She cocked her head. "You aren't?"

"No."

He'd taken this a good deal better than she'd expected a son finding his mother kissing a man who'd not been his father might. "Oh." Christina fought a giddy urge to smile.

"I'm angry with you."

That managed to quash her all too short-lived relief. "Oh," she repeated, that single, useless syllable. And she deserved his anger. What son would not take offense at his mother kissing a man as she'd been?

"I'm angry because you're going to marry someone other than Martin."

"You… want me to marry Mr. Phippen?" She managed to whisper the question through the shock of that revelation. "I… But you don't like him," she said. "Or I thought you didn't."

Her eldest child blushed and ducked his head. "I didn't at first. But he's proven a good enough fellow. Plays with us. Doesn't lecture us." Her son paused. "He makes you smile."

Her heart alternately swelled with warmth and twisted with pain. "He does make me smile," she said softly.

"I know. And if you're going to marry anyone, well, then I want it to be someone who makes you smile, and who plays with us, and who isn't horrified when Lara spits up on his shoulder." As the babe had done to Martin almost every time he'd held the babe while going out of his way to include the child in games. "I don't want you to just marry some proper, tight-laced fellow because of us."

"Oh, Lachlan." Her heart breaking all over again, Christina dropped to a knee and touched a hand to his small shoulder, one that was also broad in so many ways it shouldn't have to be. She moved her gaze over his face. "I love you."

"I know that. That's why I think you're going to do something foolish, because Grandmother is making you feel bad about us." He implored her with his eyes. "But you don't have to feel bad about us. You don't have to marry some miserable lord who isn't going to make you smile the way Caleb makes Aunt Claire smile or Tynan makes Aunt Faye…" He paused. "Or the way *Martin* makes *you* smile."

Tears filled her eyes. "Oh, Lachlan," she said again.

"If you feel you have to marry someone, why can't it be Martin, hmm?" he asked, more than faintly pleading.

Christina sank back on her haunches. "Because it's not that simple."

"Do you care about him?"

She loved him. "Of course I do."

"He cares about you. I know it. I can see it. And he kissed you, so that means something."

It should. To her, it did. And to Martin, the man whom she'd come to care so very much about, she wagered it did, too. He wasn't a man who'd run about just kissing women he didn't carry some feelings for. She touched a finger to her lips. "Please, don't—"

Lachlan rolled his eyes. "Yeah, yeah. I know. Don't talk about it." And this time, like he was the grownup and she the child, he took her by the shoulders. "But I'm not talking about it in front of everyone. I'm talking about it to you." He pressed a little fist against her chest. "I want you to be happy again, Mama."

"I am happy, because of you and your brother and sisters," she said, brushing a curl back from his brow. It immediately sprang back into place.

Her son released a sound of annoyance. "That's not the kind of happiness I'm talking about. I mean, I was little before Da was sick. But I remember how you'd laugh and smile and *really* laugh and smile, not like what you've been doing now so we aren't sad."

Oh, God. He was even able to detect the sincerity of her smile. "When did you grow up?" she murmured, caressing his cheek.

"Over the years, Mama. You just had so much with Da that you didn't realize it."

Yes, the care of her children had largely fallen to their nursemaid, while she'd remained at her ailing husband's side.

Guilt threatened to swallow her.

"Oh, don't look like that," Lachlan said, almost desperate in his urging. "Like you feel bad because you were taking care of Da. Do you think I'd do anything but love you more because I saw how you took care of him, while still trying to smile for me, Logan, and Luna's benefit?"

A sob burst from her lips, and Lachlan immediately folded her in his arms, and they clung to each other, just holding on. "Please, don't cry," he begged.

Wiping a trembling hand over her tear-stained cheeks, she then reached that same shaking palm for her son's face. "I'm just happy," she said, her voice catching and tears once more threatening.

His brow scrunched up. "It doesn't *look* like you're happy."

"Sometimes tears are the happy kind."

When he continued to look dubiously back, she laughed softly and pulled him in close for another hug.

A short few moments later, her son, who waffled between being a wise beyond-his-years gentleman and a small boy, proved more the latter by wiggling out of her embrace, his cheeks pink. "What will you do?"

Her heart paused. "What will I do?"

Because the fact remained, marriage was necessary. She'd come to realize Martin had been correct. She deserved happiness and had resolved to find it again for herself, and she'd been set with his words in mind to make a new life.

Only now, she wanted that new life with him.

"Mama?" Lachlan urged, pulling her away from those distracted musings. "What are you going to do about

Martin? Will you marry him?"

What was she going to do? Or, what did she want to do? "I... don't know," she answered truthfully.

Her son's face fell. "But we *liiiiike* him. *I* like him."

Yes, he'd been more reluctant to come around than his siblings. "I know, and I like him, too—"

"Then there are no buts. You just marry him."

Marry Martin. Her heart sped up, knocking excitedly against her chest at the mere prospect, and yet...

"I don't know if Martin wants to marry me."

Her son looked at her like she'd sprouted a second head. "Of course he wants to marry you. He kissed you."

This time, her cheeks went warm. "Shh," she reminded, pressing a fingertip against her lips. "And also, sometimes a kiss is... just a kiss."

Martin's hadn't felt like just a kiss. It had tasted of joy and love and the future she ached for with him.

Lachlan drew back, his brow creased with his befuddlement. "Why would anyone kiss someone they don't like?"

"It's not that he doesn't like me. And I'm not even saying necessarily that the kiss didn't matter..." She was rambling. "I'm saying sometimes it doesn't, but sometimes it does," she said when his brow dropped in further consternation.

She was making a mess of this.

Martin was a confirmed bachelor, as he'd said, in his thirties, who'd never considered a family for himself. As such, wrapping his brain around that would be entirely different than Martin wrapping his heart around her children as he had. Christina tried again. "I'm saying I don't know how Martin feels about a future with me." With all of them.

She, however, omitted that latter part for her son.

"Then you have to ask him." A frantic glimmer lit his eyes as he looked beyond her shoulder to the doorway. "You have to ask him before Grandmother runs him away."

Yes, that was certainly what awaited Martin.

In fact, he'd already likely been sent off by now.

Would he just leave without saying goodbye?

In the end, the inevitable knock came.

Rap, rap, rap.

In unison, her and Lachlan's heads swung toward the front of the room.

Rap, rap—

"Grandmother," Lachlan whispered as the dowager baroness let herself in swiftly enough to pick up traces of those last syllables.

"Yes, your grandmother," she said with such ice dripping from those three words that Lachlan sidled closer to Christina.

Coming to her feet, Christina rested a protective hand on his shoulder, squeezing, and looked across the room at her mother.

Had her mother's voice ever been anything but frosty and empty of emotion? Christina searched her mind for a moment in her past when her mother had ever been kind or her tones warm… and came up empty.

"Take yourself off now, Lachlan. I wish to speak to your mother."

Her son instantly made to go, but Christina gripped his arm a touch tighter. "Do not speak to my son so," Christina said quietly, her demand bringing both her mother's and son's eyebrows skyrocketing.

"I speak to him as I do any other person, Christina," her mother returned impatiently, more than slightly confused.

"But he's not any other person," Christina said, stepping forward and placing herself between her scared son and last living parent. "He's your grandson and a little boy. As such, do not order him about as you do…" Everyone. The servants. Her own children.

The tight line of her mother's lips hinted at her barely contained fury for being so called out.

Christina had unsettled her. Good, taking the wind out of her sails before their meeting about what had really brought her mother here could only be helpful for Christina.

"Very well," her mother finally relented, and then shockingly, when her mother again directed her next words at Lachlan, she did so in a gentler way. "Lachlan, dear, will you please step out a moment and allow me to speak with your mother?"

Her son hesitated before nodding. Except, instead of taking his immediate leave, he looked to Christina. "You'll be all right?" he whispered for her ears only.

Christina offered a tiny nod. "I promise," she mouthed, making a discreet X upon her chest.

As he padded slowly across the room, she realized her words hadn't been issued as empty assurances for a nervous little boy. Christina *would* be all right.

Regardless of whatever else unfolded this day, she'd stood up to her mother in defense of her children and had put an end to her bullying of at least them. She'd also resolved to not rush into the future her mother wished for her, but rather to seek out the one she wanted for herself.

And she wanted Martin.

If he'd gone, or if he wished for a different future than the one she hoped for, then she would deal with the loss of him and that dream the same way she had the other broken dreams in her life.

Lachlan paused at the doorway, casting a glance back.

Christina smiled and lifted her hand in a light wave meant to reassure.

Her son smiled widely, both cheeks dimpling, and then, with a little wave of his own, he left.

The moment Lachlan had gone, the dowager baroness didn't waste any time. She set off on an immediate pace, striding back and forth across the long bedroom. "I cannot *believe* you have done this. You of all people," her mother railed.

Christina stood by the bed, her hands folded on her lap, like she was the child who'd oft been scolded for sins and crimes of which she still could not remember. Only, she wasn't that scared child. Not anymore.

A sharp laugh escaped her mother, who apparently required no input from Christina at this point and was rather content to let her recriminations flow freely. "Actually, perhaps I should have. You, who insisted on wedding a poor merchant, would also throw yourself like some wanton at a builder."

Fury cast a red haze over her vision, briefly blinding. "How dare you?" she seethed, and how dare Christina for not having called her mother out long before this moment? "I loved my husband, and Patrick was a good man, a far better person than you or Father ever were and could ever hope to be," she said.

Either the words, or the sharpness of them, wrung a gasp from her mother.

But Christina, for the first time since Patrick's passing, had found her voice and thrilled in using it to put this woman in her place.

"And Mr. Phippen, he is also a *good* man," Christina continued, for the past was the past, and now there was a new man whom she'd come to love, and he was being disparaged by a woman who, with her past crimes and sins and the ugliness of her soul, was unworthy to be in the same room as him. "Martin is a *very* good man," Christina reiterated. She took a deep breath and shared the last piece that she knew would set her mother off. "He is also one I care very deeply about." Only, that was not all. "I love him," she added softly. "I love him very much."

Her mother strangled on a half sob and then clutched at her throat, choking. "Love him? You don't even know him. He is a stranger."

"Many marriages are made in even shorter times than that which Martin and I have shared." Some were even made among strangers, as her sister's had been. "Need I remind you about Claire?" she delighted in pointing out anyway.

"I don't need you to remind me of Claire," she said crisply.

Christina opted to do so anyway. "Claire knew her husband hardly at all when she set off to wed him." When Christina had been about to lose her husband, Claire had rushed off to marry a stranger, who'd proven to be Caleb, the same man her sister was hopelessly in love with now. "And Faye knew Tynan even less—"

"Do you expect me to rejoice in these examples?" her mother hissed. "These rushed marriages between your sisters and men so far beneath them in birthright?"

Christina stared at her mother for a long moment. Was it a wonder love should have that effect on this heartless woman? "I spent my life not knowing whether to fight for your love," she said softly, "or hate you for who you are." The mother and person she'd been incapable of ever being. "Only to find that I don't feel either way. Rather, I feel sorry for you, Mother."

Her mother scoffed. "What do you have to pity me for?"

"I feel badly that you don't know what it is to *truly* love."

"Bah. Love." Her mother let that word fall from her tongue like she'd been poisoned by the mere mention of it. "And your Mr. Phippen, the builder," her mother went on, turning the conversation back to the only thing she cared about in this instant. "You speak of love with him." She strode furiously over to Christina, her skirts whipping angrily, and a wind rose up suddenly outside, battering the window and seeming to cast a more ominous look on the older woman. "But does he love you?"

Christina paused, and her mother, a mistress of detecting weakness and grinding a person under her heel, did what she did best—she cast doubt and uncertainty.

"Has he spoken of loving you?" her mother pressed.

"It isn't your business what Martin and I have shared," she said as calmly as she was able.

Her mother was unrelenting. "Has he even *offered* for

you? Has he given any indication that he wants anything more than to toss your skirts up and take his pleasures in a momentary diversion?"

She colored. "That is not what it's been between Martin and I, and he has—"

"He has what?" her mother cut her off. "Played with your children? That doesn't mean he wishes to marry you, Christina." She sounded exasperated at Christina's naïveté.

It isn't naïveté, a voice silently screamed in her head, but the dowager baroness continued wreaking her usual havoc.

"Your children and *you*, *Christina*, will be a burden to any man you eventually wed."

Christina winced and turned her face away from that sharp condemnation.

But her mother wasn't done. She wouldn't be until she'd accomplished a total annihilation of her daughter. "You think I'm cruel for saying as much, but you *know* in your heart of hearts that it is true. They are four mouths." Her mother shot four fingers up. "Two Seasons." She added another two digits. "And that's *if* your daughters don't require additional Seasons." By her tone, her mother had already ruled that likely. Her mother gave her a pitying look, one that sent warning bells chiming. "Has he come to you?"

"I'm certain he hasn't had time to—"

"No, he hasn't," the dowager baroness agreed. "Because he's already on his way."

And her heart, which had sung so many times these past days because of Martin, struck a discordant pitch. *On his way...?* What was her mother saying?

"Leaving," her mother said, confirming that Christina

had, in fact, spoken those hollow words aloud.

"You made him go," she whispered, balling her hand into a fist and raising and then lowering that shaking limb. Lost. At sea. "You ordered him gone."

"I asked him, Christina," her mother said quietly. "That is altogether different. He saw that it was best for each of you that he leave. I merely suggested it, but he acknowledged it needed to be done for your happiness."

"My happiness." She knew her breathless echo after echo were meaningless utterances, and yet, she wasn't capable of more in that moment.

Through the agony of loss, fury penetrated, a living, breathing force that she welcomed, drinking deeply of that cup and giving an outlet to the pain of Martin's departure. "How dare you speak about my happiness?" she hissed. "You have never cared about me or my happiness. Or, for that matter, that of any of your children. Not your grandchildren. You are a selfish, coldhearted woman with a shriveled soul, and that raises the very dubious possibility that you were even born with one in the first place."

The color leached from the dowager baroness' cheeks. "Christina—"

"Get out," she said quietly.

"How dare you?"

Striding across the room, Christina grabbed the door handle in shaky fingers, yanked the door open. "I dare quite easily. Now, go."

Her mother remained rooted to the floor for a moment, tipping her chin up a notch, bringing her shoulders back a fraction, and then, with all the stiff form Queen Charlotte herself couldn't have evinced, she made a march and left.

Christina pushed the door shut firmly but quietly behind her, the metallic click the only hint of sound echoing in the quiet.

But then, her mother had already gotten what she wanted. Martin had gone, and the possibility—nay, the dream of him—as a husband for Christina was gone. As such, any words Christina might hurl at her mother, albeit cruel words but also true ones, would be ineffectual arrows landing no mark upon the other woman.

Christina remained there, frozen, before all the life and energy slipped from her muscles, rendering her legs useless.

With a shuddering gasp, she collapsed against the doorway, resting her forehead atop that panel.

Then the tears came. Great big, gasping heaves that threatened to rip her apart. Sliding onto the floor, Christina lay with her back against the door as she gave herself over to the cry she so desperately needed.

She loved him.

She wanted him in her life. She wanted him in her children's lives.

But she knew one person loving another wasn't enough.

She stilled. Perhaps he'd gone because he'd not known she cared about him? Perhaps if she told him how she felt, that might matter to him and how he felt about her?

Energized by the possibility of it, Christina scrambled to her feet and took off flying across the chambers.

Perhaps her pride would be crushed, but it had been so broken before, and she'd come to appreciate that pride was a useless, empty companion.

Skidding to a stop at the armoire, she wrenched the

doors wide and fished around inside.

Rap, rap.

There came a firm, sharp knock, followed by the click of the door opening, briefly interrupting her search.

Christina yanked the green wool Faye had gifted her from the back of the armoire and spun around with the garment in her hand.

"I've already told you I want you go—*oh*." That harsh order ended on a breathless sigh as Martin closed the door behind him.

He was here.

Her heart thundered.

He'd not gone.

"You want me to go?" Martin drawled, leaning against that heavy oak panel.

"No!" she exclaimed. The hand holding her cloak shot out, and she waved the fabric in his direction. "I thought you had left," she explained, her voice breaking all over again.

Martin padded across the room, and as he did, she devoured the sight of him, scarcely daring to believe he was real, trying to reconcile his presence with the absolute confidence of her mother's insistence that he'd gone.

Martin stopped just a pace away. His eyes moved over her face, and with an infinite tenderness, he brushed the rough pad of his thumb over her swollen cheek. "You've been crying."

As her eyes ached from the copious amount of tears she'd shed, she didn't even bother with the attempt to deny it. She merely nodded.

Then he let his hand fall, and she wanted to weep all over again at the loss of his touch.

"Because of me."

She nodded.

"Because I got you caught by your children and mother…"

She realized then what she'd agreed to. "No!" She grabbed his hands. "Not that. Never that. I thought you'd gone," she said. "I… was told you'd left."

"Your mother?"

She nodded. "Yes. She said she had spoken with you."

His lips quirked in a wry grin. "More like *to* me. In fairness, she did most of the speaking. She made it beyond clear that she wanted me gone. Your mother, she's not much of a listener."

She flashed a droll smile of her own. "No, she's not."

"She guessed that I've come to care about you. She asked me to do what would bring you happiness."

Christina clasped a hand to her throat. "You… care about me?" she whispered.

A gentle smile formed on his hard lips again. His hand came up, and she held her breath, but he merely brushed one of her curls back behind her ear, his gaze lingering on the strand he held. "That's really so surprising?"

"Yes." Because she loved him. Because deep down, she yearned for him to feel the same way. And yet, caring for her and her children was altogether different than loving them.

Except, something he'd said prior, something she'd failed to concentrate on until now, reached her. Christina's heart paused, and she dampened her mouth. "What would she have heard had she been listening?"

"She asked that I do the right thing," he said quietly, his gaze fixed with hers.

As in leaving…

"And I promised I would. She thanked me, but she assumed I had agreed to leave, Christina." His voice grew thick.

Her heart stilled.

"What she failed to realize was that I wasn't promising to leave, but rather to stay… because I know you fill me and my heart with more happiness than I've ever known, and I've seen you smile, and I love your smile. I love your children, even when they're up to their antics." He laughed and then corrected himself. "Especially when they're up to mischief."

Christina's reciprocal laugh melded with a sob.

His voice grew more impassioned, more roughened by emotion, as he lowered his brow to hers and looked down at her. "And I think I make you happy. It's because of that hope that I remained. I told your mother I cared about you, but it's more than that. I love you. And if I'm not wrong, and you feel the happiness I do when we are together, then I'll stay, and if—"

Weeping, Christina tossed her arms around him. Martin's came up, and he instantly folded her close.

"I love you," she rasped, gripping his cheeks and bringing his face down so she might kiss his lips. "I love you so very much, and I didn't know how my heart would take losing you, too."

A pained groan spilled from his lips, and he kissed her hard. "And it won't have to," he vowed. "Because I'm not ever leaving you, Christina. This is forever."

Forever.

As he claimed her lips, this time in a gentler kiss, she smiled, eager for the future that awaited them together.

Epilogue

Martin had asked Christina to marry him.

He had.

Lost in so much love of her and overwhelmed by the moment, he'd been consumed only by those emotions and the hungering to spend the future with her.

But he'd been hasty.

There'd been other business to attend.

More important than all previous business meetings he'd taken part in.

As such, Martin approached it with all the somberness befitting such gravity.

Arms clasped behind him, he stared at the audience of three. Well, five, if one included Christina and baby Lara.

It was a very serious, solemn-looking army.

Lara, precious babe that she was, didn't grasp the severity of the situation.

Alternately batting at her mother and clapping her hands, she smiled at Martin.

Martin returned that smile.

"Ahem." Lachlan cleared his throat loudly, redirecting Martin's attention back to the three assembled children before him.

"My apologies," he murmured, lowering his head deferentially.

And then, among the Thacker siblings able to stand and talk, it was Luna who cracked. The little girl giggled, shifting back and forth excitedly on her feet.

Logan gave his younger sister a look and whispered something to her.

The girl squirmed and then erased her smile, replacing it with a more serious line.

Catching her eye, Martin winked.

Luna giggled once more, hiding that restored grin behind her little palm.

Lachlan at last commanded the silent exchange. "Now, we come to the reason for your audience, Mr. Phippen."

"It's just Martin," Logan reminded him.

"Shh, we're conducting business," Lachlan muttered.

"But we voted to call him Martin when he came last week," Luna interrupted, and she looked to Martin. "Uncle Caleb is from America, and he told us about voting, and he said that men vote, but women should vote to, I said, and he agreed, and he said someday he suspects—"

"Luna!" Lachlan said impatiently.

At their side, a still-silent Christina smiled, hiding that grin in the top of Lara's dark curls. She and Martin caught each other's eyes and shared a look.

"I love you," she mouthed.

"I love you," he returned, equally soundless.

"Ahhhhem." Lachlan called the meeting to order for a second time. "As I was saying, we are here to discuss the reason for your audience. It has come to our attention that you love our mother. Is this true?"

"More than anything."

"More than all the buildings you designed." Luna shot a finger out.

"Every single one, plus the ones I have not built combined," Martin vowed in solemn tones.

"What about more than all of Claire's cook's sweets combined?" Logan demanded.

"I love the four of you *and* your mother more than all of both of your aunts' cooks and all the baked goods in England and the world," he amended, earning an approving nod from Lachlan.

"More than winning snowball fights?" Lachlan asked, pointing at Martin's chest.

Martin lowered his head once more and touched a hand to the place where his heart beat. "I'd happily concede every match for the opportunity to be part of your family."

Christina's audible sigh reached him.

Lachlan captured his chin between his thumb and forefinger and rubbed it, all the while contemplating Martin. "Very well." He let his arm fall and extended his palm toward Martin. "You may marry my mother and be part of the family."

No sooner had that concession been granted than jubilant cries went up as Christina's children swarmed him, collectively hugging him, and as he returned their welcoming embraces, and Christina and Lara joined in, his laughter melded with theirs.

The End

If you enjoyed, *It Happened One Winter* be sure and check out the other books in the *Scandalous Affairs* series:
A Groom of Her Own
Taming of the Beast
My Fair Marchioness
It Happened One Winter

Want to know the story of Christina's brother Tristan, the Earl of Bolingbroke and his wife, Poppy?
Courting Poppy Tidemore

And be looking for my next book, coming February 22, 2022 when I return to my *Heart of Duke* series!
To Catch a Viscount

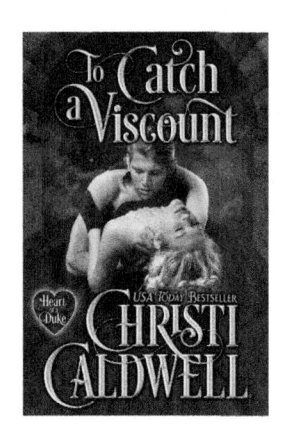

Miss Marcia Collins's cameo-perfect life is destroyed when scandal leaves her standing alone at the altar on her wedding day. Her heart shattered, she decides to embrace her ruined reputation and explore every forbidden pleasure. All she needs is a little help from her long-time friend—and society's most wicked rogue—Andrew Barrett, Viscount Waters.

Andrew tried his hand at love and lost badly, and has no interest in marriage or respectability. Nonetheless, even he knows he should avoid Marcia and her harebrained attempts to embark on a life of impropriety. Andrew, however, has never done what he's supposed to do, nor can he stand about twirling his sword cane while Marcia dabbles in forbidden pleasures without him.

When they push the boundaries too far, Marcia and Andrew must determine whether old secrets will keep them apart, or newfound love can forge a path back to a respectable, shared future.

Biography

Christi Caldwell is the bestselling author of historical romance novels set in the Regency era. Christi blames Judith McNaught's "Whitney, My Love," for luring her into the world of historical romance. While sitting in her graduate school apartment at the University of Connecticut, Christi decided to set aside her notes and try her hand at writing romance. She believes the most perfect heroes and heroines have imperfections and rather enjoys tormenting them before crafting a well-deserved happily ever after!

When Christi isn't writing the stories of flawed heroes and heroines, she can be found in her Southern Connecticut home with her courageous son, and caring for twin princesses-in-training!

Visit www.christicaldwellauthor.com to learn more about what Christi is working on, or join her on Facebook at Christi Caldwell Author, and Twitter @ChristiCaldwell!

Printed in Great Britain
by Amazon